"Who ever heard of a vampire working at a 7-Eleven?" I muttered, standing at the Slurpee machine.

Technically, it wasn't a 7-Eleven. It basically amounted to the same thing and business in this location. You'd think the owners would have clued into the fact this particular road thirty minutes off the highway wasn't the best place to put such a store.

I was dressed in a green apron and doing double duty restocking the shelves and working the counter since my partner, David, was doing approximately jack and shit to help me. David Treme was a reasonably good-looking blond-haired Caucasian man who was presently doing his "Randal from Clerks" impression by reading a porn magazine as I did his job for him. This was doubly ridiculous because he was technically my slave.

Heavy on the "technically."

"Hell, Peter, who ever heard of a Black vampire?" David said, not bothering to look up.

I stopped struggling with the Slurpee machine. "There have been plenty of Black vampires."

"Name four."

"Eddie Murphy in *Vampire in Brooklyn*, Aaliyah in *Queen of the Damned*, Blade, and Blacula."

"Blade is a half-breed; he doesn't count."

"Hey hey, can it with the racism," I said, frowning. "Some of us started as half-breeds."

David lowered his magazine. "Speaking of which, when are we going to seal the deal?"

I grimaced. "Could you not call it that?"

Special thanks to my wife Kat, Jeffrey Kafer, David Niall Wilson, David Dodd, and others who helped me bring this project to fruition.

Macabre Ink is an imprint of Crossroad Press Publishing
For information address Crossroad Press at 141 Brayden Dr., Hertford, NC 27944
www.crossroadpress.com

First edition

STRAIGHT OUTTA FANGTON

by C. T. Phipps

MACABRE
Ink

Introduction

I love me some vampires.

I began my love affair with the undead with *The Lost Boys* on television when I was ten years old. They were unlike the images of vampires I'd had in the back of my head from cultural osmosis. They were cool, they were nasty, and they were rebellious.

Later, I would become a fan of Anne Rice's creations and for the next decade would enjoy just about anything vampire related: *The Blade Trilogy, Buffy the Vampire Slayer, The Dresden Files, From Dusk Till Dawn, Fever Dream, Forever Knight, John Carpenter's Vampires, Near Dark, Necroscope, True Blood, Underworld, Vampire: The Masquerade,* and even the Anita Blake novels before they turned into erotica.

But unfortunately, vampires lost some of their cultural panache, partly because the romantic vampire genre has portrayed so many bloodsuckers as merely harmlessly eccentric. This isn't to dis the romantic vampire—it's a trope for a reason—but the trope started to occupy the majority of headspace in fans' minds. People forgot that vampires, as cool and sexy as they might sometimes be, are monsters.

This doesn't mean there hasn't been some great vampire fiction in recent years. *Byzantium, Only Lovers Left Alive,* and *What We Do in the Shadows* are some of my favorite vampire movies of all time. I'm also of the mind that the vampire will never die as a creature, the same way the superhero will continue being a major part of our cultural heritage well into the twenty-first century. They're just too good a metaphor for too many things.

Straight Outta Fangton is my attempt to throw my hat into the world of the undead. When Crossroad Press contacted me about doing a series for them, I was pleasantly surprised. I was just off working on my existing series in *The Rules of Supervillainy* and wanted to do something different. Having written a book that sends up all the tropes of superheroes and their bizarre relationship with the world while telling a serious, coherent story, I thought I'd do the same for the Nosferatu.

I don't think I send up this genre quite as successfully because the vampire is fundamentally a terrifying figure, but I think it's still pretty damn entertaining.

Special thanks to my wife Kat, Jeffrey Kafer, Jim Bernheimer, Mike Gibson, and others who helped me bring this project to fruition.

CHAPTER ONE

"Who ever heard of a vampire working at a goddamn 7-Eleven?" I muttered, standing there fiddling with the Slurpee machine.

Technically, it wasn't a 7-Eleven. It was a Qwik & Shop, which basically amounted to the same thing and was the fifth sort of this business in this location. You'd think the owners would have clued into the fact this particular road thirty minutes off the highway wasn't the best place to put such a store.

I was dressed in a green apron and doing double duty restocking the shelves and working the counter since my partner, David, was doing approximately jack and shit to help me. David Treme was a reasonably good-looking blond-haired Caucasian man who was presently doing his "Randal from *Clerks*" impression by reading a porn magazine as I did his job for him. This was doubly ridiculous because he was technically my slave.

Heavy on the "technically."

"Hell, Peter, who ever heard of a Black vampire?" David said, not bothering to look up.

I stopped struggling with the Slurpee machine. "There have been plenty of Black vampires."

"Name four."

"Eddie Murphy in *Vampire in Brooklyn*, Aaliyah in *Queen of the Damned*, Blade, and Blacula."

"Blade is a half-breed; he doesn't count."

"Hey hey, can it with the racism," I said, frowning. "Some of us started as half-breeds."

David lowered his magazine. "Speaking of which, when are we going to seal the deal?"

I grimaced. "Could you not call it that?"

"What? You'd prefer I term it something more erotic? I thought all vampires were bisexual."

I blinked once. "No, David."

"Well, that's disappointing."

I sighed. "Well, we're all learning new things about our condition, aren't we?"

When Thoth had approached me about the possibility of becoming a vampire, he'd more or less made it sound like becoming undead would be one long party. Since the Great Economic Collapse when the Vampire Nation had bailed out the country, vampires had moved back from friendly body-glitter types to ruthless sexy badasses again. Thoth, who lived a life between Jay Z's and Dracula's, certainly made it work.

Thoth might have mentioned I was expected to work his way up from the bottom and make my own fortune, though. Honestly, there were times I regretted his making me a vampire. I didn't have any problem with the liquid diet, vulnerability to sunlight, or occasional homicidal urges, but being his servant had come with the perks. Now I was back to the same sort of work I'd been doing before Iraq, especially since my exile from New Detroit.

"I'm just saying, I'm ready for the next step." David shrugged his shoulders. "How long have we been friends?"

"Too long by my estimation," I said, giving up on fixing the Slurpee machine.

"So maybe it's time you made me undead."

"You've only been my servant for a few months, David."

"That's long enough."

I rolled my eyes and went back to the cash register, biting my tongue about how I'd been Thoth's servant for four years. David knew that and didn't care. I decided, instead, to point out the systemic concerns. "It's a bit more complicated than just changing whoever I want. Population control is a big thing among the undead. After the explosion following the Bailout, they've seriously been cracking down on the creation of new vampires. Any one of us who changes a mortal without the local voivode's permission gets killed."

"Isn't that illegal?" David said, finally paying attention. "I mean, we're United States citizens and all."

"The half of the Supreme Court owned by vampires holds the rights of the VN sacred while the other half approves of anything that gets more vampires killed."

I turned to the seventy-year-old across the counter who'd been waiting for her Slurpee. "I'm sorry, but the machine is busted. Can I get you anything else?"

The woman sniffed the air before grabbing her handbag. "You realize you're going to Hell." It was statement rather than a question.

I paused, wondering if I should respond to the old bat. "Yes. Yes, I do."

The woman stomped out, forgetting her debit card.

I picked her card up and slipped it into the lost and found, not bothering to go after her. "Can you believe that?"

"Speaking as a bisexual man, yes," David said, shrugging. "Don't take this the wrong way, but I'm actually kind of glad you guys are the new target for the Religious Right."

"And you still want to be a vampire."

"I figure immortality and the ability to fly would make up for it."

"I just kind of float," I muttered. "That's another thing they don't mention. It turns out all of those awesome powers you see in movies take time to develop, as in centuries, and aren't nearly as cool as you'd think."

"Floating is cool."

"Hypnosis would be better."

"Isn't that like rape?" David asked, tapping the Slurpee machine and making himself a Green Turboblast™.

"What?" I said, appalled.

"You know, hypnotizing women into letting you drain their blood."

"Hell no! I mean, yes, but I wouldn't do it for that. I mean for, like, uh, convincing people to give me money or sending away my creditors."

"Isn't that like theft?"

"You're a real killjoy, David."

I was spared further conversation by Steve, the other useless employee at the Qwik & Shop, who was coming back from the bathroom. He was a six foot one, thin, pale man with long black hair, sunken eyes, and bad teeth who dressed like he'd raided Russell Brand's closet and not washed for a month.

Steve Emerson was a werewolf, something I'd only found out a month into working here when he'd dropped dead for three hours before spontaneously reviving as the police were carting him off. Apparently, resurrection was their thing unless it involved wolfsbane. Though Steve was testing it with every conceivable illicit substance known to man.

"Hey," Steve said, walking up to us and staring at us.

David and I exchanged a glance.

A few moments passed.

"Uh, Steve?" I asked.

"Yeah?" Steve said.

"You want to move on down?" I asked, not caring where he went as long as it was away from me.

"I have something to tell you," Steve said.

I really hoped it was that he was quitting, but suspected he'd forget even if he did. Then again, it wouldn't make sense for him to quit since he was my boss. Yes, Steve was the manager, and not me. Goddammit, how far had I fallen that I gave a shit about that? I was actually starting to miss Baghdad.

"What is it?" David asked.

"Don't encourage him," I said. "He's on meth right now."

"Heroin, cocaine, bath salts, PCP, and several new pharmaceutical concoctions," Steve said, smiling. "It's a well-balanced mixture all canceling each other out."

"Jesus," David said. "How are you not dead again?"

I flinched at the name Jesus, which was awkward since I was still nominally Christian and hadn't taken the whole "vampires are damned before God" thing all that seriously. It had also altered my swearing, as I could take the Lord's name in vain but not actually call to him. "Actually, I'd be more concerned about how Steve is able to *afford* all the shit he puts in his system."

"I'm a millionaire," Steve said. "My great-great grandmother was Betty Crocker."

"I'm pretty sure Betty Crocker wasn't a werewolf," I said. "We'd have been able to taste the difference."

David, however, bought it hook, line, and sinker. "Why are you working here, then?"

"Because I spend all my money on drugs," Steve said, shrugging. "Anyway, you and David are like gay vampires, right?"

"You're about half-right," I said, remembering another reason why I disliked Steve.

"About the vampire or the—" Steve started to say.

"Just tell us what you wanted to say," I said. I wondered how much of Steve's addled-drug-user act was just that—an act.

Steve stuck his thumb over his shoulder and gestured back at the bathrooms. "There's a dead girl in the bathroom."

I blinked.

So did David.

"You might have opened with that," I said, pulling out my cellphone to call the cops. "Any sign of how she died?"

"Well, she's getting back up," Steve said, shrugging. He grabbed a candy bar from the front rack and started eating it in front of me.

I stopped dialing my cellphone. "Are you going to pay for that?"

"No," Steve said, chewing as he talked.

"So she's a werewolf?" David asked, all too fascinated by all this.

"No, she's one of your kind," Steve said. "That's why I brought it up. I figure when she wakes up, she's going to probably kill whoever goes in the ladies room, so we should probably lock her up until daylight and then then drag her out into the road."

"You can't do that!" I said, horrified. "That's murder."

"Can't kill what's already dead," Steve said, finishing his candy bar and dropping the wrapper on the ground. "No offense."

"Quite a bit taken," I said, appalled.

I tried to think of who could be so horrifyingly reckless and stupid to turn a mortal in the bathroom and then abandon them to whatever fate awaited them. Vampires tended to awaken extremely hungry, Steve wasn't wrong about that, and the local police had a "shoot first, never ask questions" policy when dealing with the undead. It was like being Black with a little more Black. Believe you me.

Searching my memories of the customers who'd come in the past couple of hours, I couldn't think of anyone who particularly stood out. Then again, that was kind of the point of being a vampire—we didn't look any different from anyone else. The inhuman beauty and pale skin thing was another invention of Hollywood, one for which I was very grateful.

"David, I need you to get all the security feeds for tonight," I said, taking off my apron and getting the spare key for the women's bathroom.

"You sure I should be—" David started to argue.

"Do it!" I snapped and exercised my will.

David's eyes widened and he immediately went to work, following my command. I immediately felt guilty about doing that to my friend, but this was a situation where it was justified. I hadn't been kidding about vampires and population control. It was generally agreed that there should only be one vampire for every hundred thousand humans, and given New Detroit had about two thousand Undead Americans, that wasn't exactly working out.

The Old Ones in the Vampire Nation, as a result, had made a not-so-unofficial decree that there was to be some serious population pruning. Anyone not over the age of a hundred was to be killed for the slightest offense. It had worked, after a fashion, since this had immediately resulted in the majority of people my age plotting ways they could off the Old Ones. I'd even fought in the Network Riots that had gotten a lot of my friends killed—I'd also fought on the Old Ones' side. None of that boded well for the girl in the bathroom's survival.

"Hey, are you just going to abandon your post?" Steve said as I walked past him.

"Yeah," I said. "Yeah, I am."

"Well, consider yourself fired!" Steve called back after me.

"Can you imagine someone else actually giving a shit about working here?" I called back, reaching the bathroom door. The newly reborn vampire inside hadn't ripped the door off the hinges, so that was a good sign.

Steve paused. "Shit, right, you're rehired."

"Yeah, well, I'm going to need the night off," I muttered. "I'll make it up, though."

"If you say so." Steve had already started eating another candy bar.

As I started to unlock the door, it occurred to me it was very strange Steve knew about a dead woman being reborn in the bathroom. The thought abandoned me as soon as I had it, though, because I could hear sounds of feminine agony and torment from the other side.

It was a sound that reminded me of a roadside bomb that had gone off while a bus full of mothers bringing their children home from a soccer game had been passing us. That had been another reason why I'd been glad to become a vampire.

Vampires didn't dream.

Opening the door, I peered inside the room and saw that water was starting to pool on the white tile floor where the newly created vampire had ripped out a sink and tossed it to the side. The mirrors were smashed and had little bits of blood from where her fists hadn't fully transitioned into the rock-hard granite they would later become.

The Qwik & Shop women's restroom had three green stalls and a scent of haphazardly applied bleach and disinfectant coming from everything. It didn't entirely eliminate the smells of humans going about their business, but weirdly, vampire nostrils didn't register that sort of thing as innately bad. It wasn't *good*, mind you, but our entire brain chemistry was rewired to smell and hear things differently.

The newly reborn vampire was currently on the ground in the fetal position with her arms around her legs. She was a pretty, frizzy-haired Black woman who reminded me a bit of Nathalie Emmanuelle, the actress who played Daenerys's assistant on *Game of Thrones.* The woman was dressed far too nicely for this place with an expensive leather coat and business suit dress. Both of which were getting drenched now.

Steve hadn't been lying. It was obvious she was going through the beginnings of the rebirth. I still remembered my experience with it and how utterly painful it had been. That had been when I'd had my creator with me to suppress the agony of my transformation as well as feed me fresh blood. Without your creator or enough blood to make the transformation go smoothly, it was damned near impossible to survive the event with your sanity intact.

The worst cases became draugr, what most people thought zombies were. They were mindless creatures that craved the flesh of the living. The few cases of families getting ripped to shreds and eaten had done wonders for the undeads' reputation in America, I can tell you that. Whoever had abandoned her like this was a monster.

Lifting my hands, I approached her slowly. "OK, I don't know how to do this, but I'm going to do my best. Don't be afraid, you're just becoming a vam … OK, that's terrible. Listen, I'm going to get you some blood and it's going to be A-OK. Just stay calm and try to—"

I was interrupted in my speech by her screaming as her fangs burst through from where her canines had been.

"Ouch, I hate that part," I said, taking a moment to think about where I could take her.

The hospital was a horrible choice, as many people had found out when they'd taken hungry vampires to places filled with vulnerable prey that triggered all of their predatory instincts.

An idea hit me.

"OK," I said, reaching down to take her arm. "We're going to go for a ride. I'm going to—"

The woman interrupted me by leaping up and sinking her fangs into my shoulder, tearing into my flesh to drink my blood.

Ah hell.

CHAPTER TWO

Having my shoulder torn out was pleasant. No, scratch that—it was a mind-blowingly awesome experience, like getting the best high you could imagine combined with your first girlfriend showing you what it's like to get a blow job. That's another part of being a vampire that is both cool and horrifying. When you bite a human being or another vampire, it's *always* sexual.

I hadn't been entirely truthful to David regarding what vampire feeding was like. While your sexuality didn't change, the simple fact was blood was blood and anytime you took it, it was amazing. That was all sorts of confusing for me and why I preferred feeding on women. Well, *had* preferred feeding on women. Lately, I was feeding exclusively on the vampire equivalent of protein shakes and rice cakes to avoid thinking about the last time I'd fed on a human.

Sarah …

The thought of the dead girl in my arms shook me out of the buzz being fed on was giving me. Placing my hands on her face, I tried to push back but found she was already every bit as strong as me. The awareness I was possibly going to die with a goofy grin on my face allowed me to clear my head enough to think.

An idea occurred to me. She'd drunk my blood like David and was still in the process of changing. "Back off!"

Immediately, the woman pulled away and looked confused.

"Yes!" I said, holding my shoulder. "It worked."

Closing my eyes, I felt my shoulder seal up. It wasn't without cost, as I started feeling ravenously hungry almost immediately thereafter, but I wasn't bleeding out anymore either—not that we vampires bleed very much. We're more like bottles of syrup in that our contents do pour out, but very slowly. Random Vampire Factoid #11 there.

Looking at my healed shoulder, I shook my head. "Dammit, girl, this jacket was a gift!"

"Where am I?" the woman said, looking around, confused. "What's happened to me? How did I—"

I sighed and started counting on my fingers. "You're in the bathroom of the Qwik & Go, you're a vampire now, and I have no idea who but someone created you without trying to see you through the change. That's a big no-no and now I'm going to have to take you to see the voivode."

"The what now?" the woman said, suddenly doubling over in pain.

"Old Slavic word for warlord," I said, shrugging. "Shockingly, a lot of vampires are old white Eastern European types and keep the language. It's OK. As voivodes go, she's actually pretty reasonable." Which meant she'd only stake you and leave you out for the sun if you pissed her off.

Not just for kicks.

Usually.

"Oh God," the woman said. "This isn't happening."

I flinched at her use of God's name even though she didn't seem discomforted by saying it.

Strange.

"What's your name?" I asked, deciding now would be as good a time as any to ask.

"Melissa," the woman said, trying to take a breath but failing. "Melissa Morris."

Morris. Like Quincey Morris, the guy who killed Dracula?

Huh, that was an ironic name.

"What's yours?" Melissa asked, blinking a few times as if to adjust to how her sight was working.

"Peter Stone," I said, shrugging. "There's a whole bunch of ritual greetings vampires are supposed to exchange when meeting for the first time as well as a secret handshake, but I'm no good at this shit. Besides, what you really need to do is tell me who created you."

"You didn't?" Melissa said, confused.

I felt my face. *"No, I didn't do it."*

"Oh," Melissa said, frowning. "Then I have no idea who changed me. Who ... damned me."

I raised an eyebrow. "Please don't tell me you're a Jes ... J-guy freak."

"J-guy freak?"

"Vampires have issues with organized religion," I said, not adding *that isn't ours*. "Groups like the Human Rights League, Mothers against Vampires, and so on really don't give me a warm fuzzy feeling."

Melissa took a defensive tone. "You don't think vampires are—"

"Oh, you are!" I said, grimacing.

Melissa looked embarrassed. "I'm not like a fanatic. I just think it's important for humans to protect themselves."

"It's that kind of racist language that—"

That was when David stupidly chose to walk in and Melissa's eyes bulged out before she leapt for his throat.

"Stop!" I shouted.

Almost as if an invisible hand had grabbed her in midair and pulled her down, Melissa hit the ground with a thud.

David took a deep breath. "Wow, that was awesome!"

"You almost got killed!" I snapped at my servant. "Give me a heads-up when you're approaching a hungry newborn vampire."

"So ..." Melissa struggled over her next words. "Hungry. No, I don't want to drink blood, but ... I do."

David frowned and looked down. "Okay, now you're just cheating me."

"What?" I asked, looking at him.

"You're telling me the fact she's a beautiful woman has nothing to do with the fact she was made before me?"

"I found her here!" I snapped. "Also, bluntly, you've been serving me for three weeks!"

"The longest three weeks of my life! You're not the easiest guy to work with."

I stared. "That's it, you can find some other vampire to turn you."

"What?" David said, opening his mouth in horror. "You can't do that! We had a deal!"

"One you have royally—"

Melissa screamed in a mixture of rage and anguish.

I helped her up. "It's OK, we're going to get you some blood now."

Melissa hissed at David.

"Not his," I said. "You wouldn't want it anyway. He's Irish."

"Funny." David immediately straightened up, her hungry stare finally impressing on him the danger of the situation. "Oh, right, well, there's nobody on the security camera except her."

"Wait, what do you mean, nobody?"

"I'm saying they didn't show up," David said. "Someone came in and paid for some stuff but they didn't show up on film."

Well, crap. That added a whole new layer of wrong to the situation. Vampires not showing up in mirrors was another partially true bit of folklore. We did show up in mirrors, for the first century or two of life, before our images gradually faded away. If this vampire really didn't cast a reflection, then that meant he was old.

Old One old.

The Vampire Nation was a meritocracy, which was another reason why I had issues with the way things were run. It didn't matter if you were the smartest, most charismatic, most talented guy who had a brain that wasn't stuck in the Middle Ages.

You took a backseat to some old-as-dirt Orlock-looking thing that tended to think of America as a place filled with natives assaulting covered wagons, if they thought of it at all. Frankly, even the Old Ones here were getting sick of how the Ancients were treating them. This would only rile them up, as theoretically they were supposed to know better, and my bringing this girl to them would possibly get us both killed.

I needed my creator.

"Shit," I whispered, processing that. "You stay here, David. I'm going to go deal with this."

"Hell no," David said. "This is the most interesting thing that's happened in months. I'm not hanging around here to clean up the broken toilet."

"Sink," I corrected, looking down at the now huge puddle of water on the ground. "Someone should really turn that off."

David didn't take the hint.

"Fine. Call Thoth and tell him I'm coming."

I hadn't parted with my creator on good terms, what with the whole complicated cutting me off, spying on my girlfriend, and exile thing, but I still trusted him. Contrary to almost every piece of vampire lore in media history, I liked the person who made me a vampire and wanted him to succeed in his plan to make New Detroit a haven for our kind. He was a cold-blooded sonofabitch, but I could trust him with this.

Probably.

I leaned down and picked up Melissa, putting her arm around my neck while my arm was around her waist, and started to lead her past David. She snapped at him a bit, but my control over her was strong enough to keep her from doing anything stupid. Vampires who drank each other's blood tended to have a strong psychic connection, and she'd imbibed mine during her rebirth. That would give me some control for the next few days.

Possibly longer.

I really wish I'd paid more attention during Thoth's lessons.

"Okay, we're going to get you some blood. Just hang on."

The two of us headed out into the Qwik & Shop only for Steve to walk up toward us, looking pissed.

"You had better have cleaned up that water," Steve said, heedless of the fact I had a half-insane newborn in my arms. "Otherwise, it's coming out of your paycheck."

Melissa looked ready to tear his throat out before she sniffed the air, then got a disgusted look on her face as if she wanted to vomit. "What the hell is wrong with him?"

"We don't have that much time," I said dryly.

"Hey!" Steve said. "I'm cutting you a lot of slack here."

"Yes, you're just Boss of the Year. Now let me take care of this before her family sues the shit out of us."

Steve blinked rapidly. "Oh crap, get her out of here."

"Yeah. As for the sink, Betty Crocker can take care of it," I muttered, heading out through the front door and around the back.

The Qwik & Shop, as I mentioned, was thirty miles off the highway to New Detroit and well into a wooded part of Michigan where absolutely no self-respecting non-furry supernatural would venture. Being close to the woods, though, had its advantages for a vampire like me, and while it didn't have the same glamour as being able to attract the most beautiful starlets or models, it got the job done.

"Where are we going? A blood bank?" Melissa asked.

"Not quite."

"I won't feed on a person," Melissa said, then grimaced. "No matter how much I want to."

Most newborns, at least the ones who hadn't been prepped yet, didn't intend to feed on humans. The thing was, vampires could and would feed on anyone from their closest relatives to the Queen of England if they were hungry enough. The only way to keep a vampire from becoming a monster was to make sure they were adequately fed all the time. Those who starved themselves, either out of guilt or some weird form of self-control, were the most dangerous vampires.

"Just stand still," I said, letting go of her. "Don't kill anyone."

Melissa stood still and looked away from the highway, practically jumping every time a car passed by on the lonely road leading back to the highway. Enhanced senses were another part of being a newborn vampire that sucked. I had to learn to keep my television down painfully low and wear sunglasses at night for months until my body adjusted to its new limits.

"Okay." I took a deep but pointless breath. "Prepare to be astounded!"

I stretched out my hand to the woods and concentrated. I attempted to reach out with the psychic powers inherent to my condition and bring forth prey to feed this abandoned daughter of vampiredom. Nothing happened. I concentrated harder and did the Chevy Chase "na-na-na-na" chant from *Caddyshack*, waving my hand a bit.

"Oh yes, I'm astounded. Oooooh," Melissa said, staring forward.

"At least your sarcasm is returning," I said, actually glad of that.

That was when my psychic lure got a little tugging and I increased my use of it until a beautiful brown deer came out between two trees, wiggling its ears as it looked around our location. It wasn't exactly controlling a massive horde of rats or wolves, but my gift with animals was probably my most advanced one.

"Oooooh," Melissa said, sweetly. "How cute."

This was going to be awkward. "Yeah, now kill it."

"What!" Melissa said, shocked. "You can't be serious."

"What, you want to rip out some poor bastard's throat?" I said, pausing before gesturing to my neck. "You know, aside from me?"

"That was the shoulder, not the neck!" Melissa said, looking aside as she clearly struggled with her hunger. "Besides, it's not very appetizing."

"No, animals are the worst," I said, frowning. "They don't have any of the pleasure of human or vampire feeding, which is probably a good thing given how sexual that is, and they only numb the hunger. You'll still have to drink small amounts of human blood even if you own a cattle yard. Still, it's all we've got so far and you're going to need to drink if you want to be taken anywhere in public."

The deer, no longer being called by my power, turned around and started to leap away.

I extended my power again. "You, come back here! Stay!"

The deer reluctantly did so.

"I'm not touching her," Melissa said, crossing her arms. "I'm a vegetarian."

I snorted at that. "Well, prepare to be carnivored."

I walked up to the door and proceeded to lift my right hand. The ends of my fingernails grew and became razor-like claws. Many vampires could shapeshift into animals, but this was all I could manage. "Sorry about this."

I then slashed across the poor deer's throat.

Seconds later, utterly breaking my control over her, Melissa zipped from her position and tackled the deer before drinking up the blood pouring from the animal. It was an uncomfortable scene to watch since she was a messy eater and videos of those were sold as the vampire equivalent of porn. Well, alongside actual porn.

Minutes later, Melissa was licking her hands like an animal then seemed to cover her face in horror. "Oh God, what have I done?"

"Survived," I said, simply.

The allure of the deer's blood was intoxicating to me too. Healing that wound had taken a lot out of me and I wasn't at my best. If I was going to confront my creator about this, I needed to be in top form.

Melissa grimaced. "I'm still hungry."

"Yeah," I said, sighing. "It never ends."

A few minutes later, there was a small pile of dead woodland creatures down at our feet. After feeding on a rabbit or two, I was strong enough to summon another deer and the awful taste aside, it put me in top form. It also would be enough to get Melissa through the night without killing anyone.

I hoped.

I recalled the horrible experience I'd had when I'd first been reborn. Thoth was a sink-or-swim mentor, so he'd put me alone in a room with a contract killer who had killed a vampire for his human wife as part of an insurance swindle. I'd ended up tearing the man's throat out and drinking every last drop of blood I could suck from his body. I still remembered the look of rapturous joy on the man's face even as he breathed his last. Thoth had wanted me up close and personal with the downside of being undead. I liked to think I was kinder.

Melissa, who would need a new outfit before I took her anywhere, looked up from the bloody animal holocaust before her. She looked more than a little shell-shocked by her experience and I couldn't blame her. She wasn't complaining about all the cute little murdered animals around her, though, which was a plus. "So, what now?"

David came out from the store a few seconds later, carrying a yellow pad covered in what I assumed was a complete transcript of everything Thoth said. Thoth was much better at mind manipulation than I was and could even do it over the phone. He also had a lot less patience with David's idiosyncrasies.

"He wants to see you," David said, coming towards us. "As soon as possible."

"Now?" I said, licking my mouth clean and pulling out a pre-moistened wipe to clean my hands. "Now we go see my creator."

CHAPTER THREE

It didn't take long for us to get on the road, just enough time to get all of the dead animals in a garbage bag before leaving them for Steve and his friends to chow on. Oh, and to stop at a big box store to pick up some jeans and a t-shirt for Melissa to change into. There wasn't much that could be done for the little patches of blood in her hair, but that was a form of decoration where we were going.

I was driving a ten-year-old green Jeep Liberty that had a plastic-covered interior and had seen better days. David was sitting in the back, playing on his cellphone while I kept my eye on the road, trying to make sense of all this. I still couldn't wrap my head around the fact an Old One had done this to someone. Didn't those rich bastards have something better to do with their time than leave some poor girl to become a draugr?

Apparently not.

"So, what's your story, lady?" David asked, surprising me by ending our enforced silence.

"Hmm?" Melissa said, pretending not to have heard him.

"How did you get into our bathroom in the middle of an hour from the interesting part of the state?" David asked, ignoring her.

Melissa was silent and looked uncomfortable.

"It's a half hour to New Detroit and I don't want to get him started on one of his 'Greatest Hits of Gangster Rap' binges," David said.

"Because you have no taste," I said. "I could have been the next big thing in rap. Straight outta Fangton."

"But you can't rhyme worth shit," David said. "Kind of hard to be a rapper that way."

I rolled my eyes, then shook my head. "I am interested, though,

Melissa. You don't seem like you're a tourist or fleeing in terror. Those are the two kinds of people who usually get lost and end up at the Qwik & Shop."

Melissa gave a half-smile. "All right, but it seems silly now. I was going to a protest."

"A protest?" I asked.

"Against vampires."

David burst out laughing and actually put away his cellphone.

"It's not funny," Melissa said, looking out the window guiltily.

"Yeah, it's not," I said, less than happy I was travelling with a bigot. I wondered if that's why the Old One had embraced her. Sort of a spur of the moment, "Well if you hate vampires, how about you feel what it's like to be one" thing. Nah, I'd yet to meet an Old One who possessed anything approaching sentimentality. Thoth came closest, and he was as cold as ice when it came to getting what he wanted.

"Which hate group did you belong to?" David asked, showing a complete and admittedly hilarious lack of tact.

"The Human Rights League isn't a hate group," Melissa said. "It's not even anti-vampire, it's pro—"

"Human?" I finished for her.

Melissa blinked. "Oh Jesus, I never even noticed that before. It *is* a hate group, isn't it?"

"All the murders of vampires they've been suspected of involvement in would indicate that, yeah," I said.

Vampire hunting was now illegal in the United States, but that didn't stop the various secular and religious organizations of the world from doing it. Indeed, the Bailout and subsequent proliferation of vampires had made it a renaissance for killers of the supernatural. Vampires were now public figures and their resting places listed in address books.

Who could blame anyone should they accidentally catch fire or there be a random home invasion? About the only good thing was the fact it turned out most of the older organizations hated each other as much as they hated vampires, with the Mormon Mankind Fellowship currently suing the Baptist Living Souls Group for libel. I wondered how those groups would feel if they knew the Old Ones paid both of them a fairly hefty donation every year to keep them thinning the ranks of the young? Probably just cash their check and complain.

"How did you get mixed up in a group like that?" David asked, showing more interest in our newborn than was probably appropriate for a servant.

Then again, she was smoking hot, bigot or not.

"My father was a Baptist minister," Melissa said, looking uncomfortable. "He was always trying to teach me right from wrong, how to tell good versus evil, and how Jesus loved everyone but he loved some people more than others."

I winced as the J-word set my teeth on edge.

"Is something wrong?" Melissa said.

"Vampires can't stand hearing the name of holy people," David explained for me. "Jesus, Buddha, Muhammed, Saint—"

"Goddammit, David!" I shouted, almost pulling over the side of the road. "What the hell?!"

"They can swear just fine, though," David said, chuckling.

"You are the worst servant ever," I said.

"Yeah." David laughed. "I am."

Melissa blinked. "Wait, is it normal for me to be able to say Jesus and not feel anything?"

It wasn't, actually. "Not unless you're a couple of hundred years old, no. The Old Ones are immune to practically everything. They can't even be killed unless it's by another Old One."

As if they didn't get enough benefits with their superpowers and wealth, they also were truly frigging immortal.

So unfair.

"Wait, what?" Melissa said. "How is that possible?"

"Magic, duh," David explained. "Same way they can fly, turn into a bat, and summon Bambi to murder."

Melissa looked ill. "I can't believe I did that."

I found myself intrigued by her story, though. "So you're an anti-vampire protestor who gets turned into a vampire at my workplace. Are you sure you don't remember anything about your attacker?"

"No," Melissa said, her voice low. "Nothing."

There was something about her tone that made me think she was holding something back. I didn't worry about that much, though, because Thoth was very good at ferreting out these sorts of things. I wasn't too happy about having to go back to my creator with my hat in my hand, especially how we'd left things, but this was beyond my pay grade. Especially since I'd started working at the Qwik & Shop. Poor girl was probably going to get executed for getting created without permission, but there wasn't much I could do about that if the voivode decreed it. The best I could do was keep her from killing people and give her the basics on her newfound, possibly short-lived, condition.

"What's your father likely to say when he finds out you've joined the Other Side?" I asked, pretty sure the answer was going to be disown her.

"He's not going to do anything," Melissa said. "He's dead along with rest of my family."

"Vampires?" David asked.

"Car accident," Melissa said. "I'm pretty sure vampires weren't responsible for the drunk driver who hit their bus with a semi. Still, I did my very best to carry on his work."

I didn't know how to react to that. "Well, we'll be in New Detroit soon enough. We'll meet with Thoth and he'll hopefully present you to Voivode Ashura."

"And if I don't get introduced to her?" Melissa said.

"You'll be declared rogue," I said. "Then you'll be hunted by the Vampire Nation's killers, FBI, Department of Supernatural Security, and all of the hate groups that will have your name forwarded to them."

"Damn," David said. "Vampires fight dirty."

"Damn straight."

Melissa was silent for a long time and I started looking for my *Death Certificate* CD. Finally, she said, "How did you get picked to become a vampire?"

"I was selected to be Thoth's servant first."

"How did that go?"

A powerful memory overwhelmed me in that moment. I remembered standing over the dead body of my brother as he lay face up on a slab in the morgue. They hadn't even bothered to close his eyes. The technician had just called me in at three in the morning to tell me to come down and identify him. Damien had only been twenty-three and now he was just another statistic.

A part of me wanted to go out to my car, get my shotgun, and track down the sons of bitches who'd killed him. I could do it too. None of these bastards were particularly subtle, and I knew more about tactics, as well as weaponry, than all of them put together. That thought left me, though, as I knew the circumstances for Damien's death. He'd killed a member of the Detroit 88s and had bragged about it to me, acting like it wouldn't fall back on him.

Damien had never listened, to me especially, that gang culture was going to get him killed. That its time had passed, if it had ever had a time in the first place. He'd wanted so hard to have a place to fit in that he'd become like a dog to Carl "Red" Jackson, the leader of the 6th Street Knives.

If I was going to kill anyone, I should kill him.

But I didn't want to kill anyone.

That was when I sensed someone behind me, a presence that seemed to fill the empty room the morgue technician had left me in. Turning my head, I saw a handsome shaven-headed Black man who was dressed in an expensive white suit with a fedora. He wore a little ankh on his lapel, a sign used by many vampires to show who they were. He had a gold-tipped walking stick that I saw had been modified to conceal a gun, even as something told me he didn't need a weapon.

"My condolences for your loss, Mister Stone," the man spoke with a light Caribbean accent.

"Yeah, thanks."

"Do you know who I am?" he asked.

"Yeah," I said, sighing. "You're Thoth the vampire. Damien used to work for you."

"Yes," Thoth said. "He used to be my driver. Then he stole from me."

I spun around and threw a punch at him.

Thoth was beside me by the time it reached where he was, not having changed his posture in the slightest. "I do not speak of it to demean your loss or the deceased. Damien was a man who dreamed of escaping the life he was born into. The allure of wealth was too much of a temptation for him, but I knew that hiring him was a risk."

I took a deep breath, aware I was going to die if I pissed this man off and not caring. "Then why hire him?"

"Everyone deserves a chance for a better life."

"What would you know about that?"

"I was born a slave. I know everything about that."

I grit my teeth. "What do you want?"

"For one, to inform you that Carl Jackson has been found with a very large amount of cocaine and is going away for the rest of his life thanks to his prior convictions," Thoth said, his tone even. "Also, I've managed to negotiate a truce between the 88s and the Knives. Neither side will be doing any further harm to the other, and both will be employed as security at some of my lesser holdings."

The vampires had been buying up downtown and demolishing it to build their little resort town for years now. Some of the money had gone back to Detroit's people, helping them get better lives and get people back in school, but lot of it had just gone to out-of-towners. Worse, plenty of people had been displaced from their homes and sent to live in even worse accommodations than before. I wasn't a fan of the Vampire Nation as a result.

"Could have done it a little faster," I said, looking back at Damien. "My brother is dead because of their stupid fucking war."

"All wars are stupid fucking wars," Thoth said, "even the ones that need to be fought."

"You put that on a fortune cookie and someone might read it."

"I want to hire you."

I actually laughed at that, all of the bitterness of the past year flowing out in a single moment. "My brother is lying dead three feet away and you're here to offer me a job? Get out of my face, fanger."

Thoth didn't move, though. "It is because of your brother's death I was able to negotiate the truce. He was a good man whom many people liked and symbolic of the losses both sides had suffered. He died, in his own way, a hero."

"He died because Red thought it would be hilarious to send him to shoot up a bar full of thirty armed 88s without telling him they were there."

Thoth was silent. "I want to give you an opportunity to escape the life you're trapped in. To repay your debts and to live free with a chance for something even greater after you have proven yourself."

I was about to tell him to piss off when I thought about Grams and the fact that I couldn't afford to pay for her care. Mom had run out years ago and my dad was God knows where now, probably still chasing his dream of getting rich enough to come back for us. "I'm listening."

"I would like you to become my servant."

"You mean your Bloodslave." Since vampires had gone public, a lot of information had become commonly known, even if they lied out of both sides of their mouth about it.

"We don't call them that," Thoth said. "Anymore."

I was ready to walk out, but something stopped me.

"Detroit is changing, Peter, and so is the world around it. The Bailout has allowed vampires an unprecedented amount of influence and is the rock on which we may build a future as friends of humanity rather than merely its keepers. This is an opportunity for the people who live in the city as well as vampiredom as a whole. The problem is there are many people who would like to see this experiment fail and go back to the days when humans hunted us every bit as much as we hunted them."

Something about his demeanor, cold and emotionless as it was, rang true. "Why me?"

"You are man of principle," Thoth said. "When others in your neighborhood and circumstances surrendered to the allure of crime, you chose to become a soldier. When you returned, ignored and forgotten by the country you served, you struggled to remain honest. You succumb to neither alcohol nor drugs to cope with the pain in your soul."

I thought about the terrible things I'd done in the war. The kids I'd had to kill because assholes used them to throw grenades or worse. "You don't know a damn thing about me."

"Don't I?" Thoth said. "Your soul is very easy to read. It is not your nobility alone that attracts me, though. It is also your willingness to break those principles you hold dear when necessary. I know about Sergeant Matheson."

I'd shot that racist piece of shit with a gun I'd recovered from one of the many conscripts we'd been killing during the initial invasion. Matheson had been the worst sort of soldier, and long before I started seeing all the weird and freaky stuff that had turned the Iraq War into the quagmire it was (not that it'd needed any help), he'd been the first genuine monster I'd ever known. The military had never picked up on the fact I'd killed him and I knew my squad mates would never tell.

I stared at him, my mouth open. "How?"

Thoth just smiled, looking like a snake as he did so. "Like I said, your soul is very easy to read. I do not judge for that or, if I do, it is with approval. He was a murderer and a thief who would have sent your unit to its death."

I was screwed. He could burn me anytime he wanted. "What do you want?"

"I want you to drink my blood and become a half-breed. You will gain great strength, as well as the ability to heal terrible wounds and bleed less when injured. You will be able to hear my voice wherever I wish. You will help me train my new security and be my personal bodyguard for the coming few years. If it becomes necessary, you will kill those who would do me or my project harm."

"So, after my brother was killed by a gang, you want me to join a bigger, richer one."

He paused. "There's one difference."

"And that is?"

"My group wants to end the fighting. My enemies want to keep it going forever."

I stared down at my feet then my next question made a lie of any nobler motivations I might have tried to convince myself were my reason for accepting. "How much do I get paid?"

It was more than enough to buy my soul.

The entire memory flash had taken less than half a second. Picking up my CD and putting it into the player, I said, "Oh, it was nothing. He needed someone and I was available."

"Oh," Melissa said.

We arrived at New Detroit soon after.

CHAPTER FOUR

Detroit had become unrecognizable. Before he'd taken off to search for oil in South Dakota, my father had told me stories about the city during its heyday, when it was the City of Rock and Roll and money was there to be made hand over fist in the auto industry. I suspected he was exaggerating, even if my hometown was a place I'd taken pride in even during its worst years.

I wasn't sure what the Vampire Nation had done to it was an improvement. In a very real way, Detroit had gone from being a city in a severe economic downturn to a weird combination of Vegas and Manhattan. Some people described it as a kind of Vampire Dubai. The "New" in front of Detroit wasn't just for show; it was a fundamental paradigm shift and transformation of the city's soul.

The outskirts of the city were still much the same, with overcrowded, crumbling buildings and tenements in bad need of repair. Strip clubs, liquor stores, massage parlors, drug dens (since they'd legalized almost everything in Michigan), fortune tellers, occult bookstores, and more were everywhere outside of Downtown. Those weren't so different, but they catered to the out-of-town crowd now for a lot more money. The closer you got, though, the more things became *strange*. Opaque black glass towers rose from the ground alongside hotels, casinos, nightclubs, and film studios. There were only a handful of vampires, comparatively, in a city of two million, but those two hundred undead had fundamentally changed the culture of the city.

Everyone worked for vampires, either directly or otherwise, with plenty adopting their style and dress, which had led to "New Detroit Goth" becoming an actual fashion term. Those citizens who didn't get with the program and work for the undead were still influenced by them, with churches and groups like Melissa's being more common than you'd believe. There were even some sham and not-so-sham health clinics that promised simply to hypnotize your addictions away.

There weren't just vampires too, as the Bailout had opened the way for hundreds of other supernaturals to immigrate to cities, where they felt there would be more acceptance. Shapeshifters, wizards, witches, demonkin, rakshasas, tengu, and otherkind all called the city home. Many of them hated vampires more than regular humans did, but it was better to be in a place you could be yourself than live a lie, no matter how bad the company.

Melissa looked like a deer in the headlights, looking at all the strange and crazy things going on around her. I didn't blame her, since there was presently a naked goblin walking down the streets beside us, spouting beat poetry.

"Man, why don't you have a piece of this?" David said, shaking his head in amusement. "This should be your place … and mine."

"Doesn't work that way," I said, shrugging as I slowly drove down Main Street toward the Apophis resort. "Everything here is owned by twenty vampires."

"You're shitting me," David said, appalled.

I shook my head. "Nope. New Detroit is owned by twenty vampires, their servants, their dhampyr children, and whatever human or supernatural hangers-on they've chosen to work with. They also pay a tithe of their profits to the Council of Ancients back in Romania. Most of the rest live in Midtown, trying to eke out a living getting selfies taken with the locals or running whatever business they can drum up with their innate mystique. Most of the places with 'vampire' in their name are run by something else, but that's how society rolls, I guess."

It was part of the reason I'd moved out, though I hadn't expected to fall quite as far as I had. Thoth had wanted me to make my own way, but he'd been offended when I'd tried to cut him out of my life completely. Every single door in the city had promptly shut in my face and my stupid pride had kept me from apologizing. I expected him to be ecstatic when I came up to his door needing a favor. That or slam the door in my face while gloating.

He was that kind of guy.

"The top one percent of one percent of the world's wealth belongs to the undead," Melissa said. "I didn't know that wasn't vampiredom in general, though."

"Yeah, well, they saved us when China cut us off," David said, crossing his arms. "Or would you prefer to have bread lines like in the Soviet Union?"

"I heard China cut us off because they found out how much of the American economy the vampires already controlled," Melissa said.

David nodded. "I also heard the Eastern vampires arranged for China to cut us off so they could take over."

"Yeah, because when I think secret mystical capitalist conspiracies, I think communists," I said, snorting at their conspiracy theories.

David and Melissa both looked at me. Apparently, even David thought they could pull it off.

They gave the Old Ones too much credit.

"What?" I said.

Neither of them had an answer for me as we came into view of the Apophis hotel and casino. It was, in simple terms, breathtakingly beautiful. It wasn't perhaps the most original design, being essentially just a larger version of the Luxor casino in Vegas with a pair of jackal-headed sphinxes plus an amusement park built into the side, but the place was the center of New Detroit's nightlife.

When vampires came in from outside the city to hold conferences, they stayed in the Apophis. When Washington D.C. congressmen and senators came to Michigan looking for bribes, they received them here. It held the hottest acts and the hottest tables and was a place many vampires wanted to live permanently, even if it meant subordinating themselves to Thoth while they were there.

A relatively small number of religious protestors were gathered outside the casino strip walkway, only a few hundred rather than the tens of thousands that would be necessary to actually shut the place down. Indeed, there was an equally large crowd gathered around them. Some of them were counter-protestors, but a lot of them were just pissed off and very drunk vacationers looking for a fight.

"Your people?" I asked, pulling toward the Apophis's private parking lot near the side entrance.

"Yeah," Melissa said, frowning. "I expected more of them to show."

"Don't come to Hell to talk about God," David said, shrugging. "The nice part of it, at least."

"If you say so," Melissa said, disgusted. "I look forward to talking to your creator."

"I'm glad someone is."

Something in her voice told me Melissa was hiding something. I could also sense apprehension and unease through our blood connection. It was possibly just the normal fear and uncertainty of being a newborn vampire, but it felt like something else. I couldn't put it into words.

My beat-up Jeep Liberty didn't exactly fit in with the sports cars, limousines, Cadillacs, Mercedes, and Audis that filled the private parking lot. However, when one of the lot's security guards tapped on my window, I gave him a hiss with my fangs and sent him running without turning his back, bowing the entire way.

"You enjoyed that," Melissa said.

"You're damned right I did," I said, getting out of the car.

"This is all overwhelming," Melissa said. "Do you ever miss it?"

"Do I ever miss what?" I said, looking at the giant pyramid next to us. "The club sandwiches with cold Mexican beers, the ten-thousand-dollar-a-night hookers, and shirts laundered like they do in the Imperial Hotel in Tokyo?"

Melissa blinked. "Did you just quote *Johnny Mnemonic* at me?"

"Finally!" I said, startling her. "I've been making variants of that quote for years now and you're the first one to have gotten it!"

"I got it," David said, shrugging. "I just didn't give a shit. You should only quote horror movies."

I rolled his eyes. "Says the guy who thinks he looks like *Fright Night*'s Colin Farrell in the right light."

Melissa looked over David and gave a disbelieving shake of her head. "The right light being darkness?"

I laughed at her. "Hey, Sunshine, you're all right."

"Sunshine?" Melissa said.

"It seems like a good nickname with you being an enormous anti-vampire bigot and all," I said, chuckling.

Melissa muttered something about vampires not being a race

before following me into the side entrance that celebrities and other VIPs used to get into the casino. The sounds of slot machines, live music, and hundreds of people pressed together in a tiny ocean of blood bags filled the air. The air was oxygen-rich to keep the customers awake as well as their blood fresh.

Walking into the actual casino floor, the bottom of a massive pyramid-shaped chamber extending upwards for hundreds of feet, was an exhilarating experience. In the center of the chamber, a huge hologram of an ankh was projected, which reflected light in colors invisible to most humans but was a spectacular light show to the undead in the room. I could also see Thoth's penthouse hanging from the top of the pyramid, a square mansion-sized box directly under the crystal apex suspended by unbreakable steel cables.

Looking at the sights before me, I took a deep breath. "You want to know whether I miss it? Really? Well, the answer is, yeah, sometimes."

That was when a fat man in khaki pants and a flowered shirt pointed at me. "Oh my God, honey, look! It's Forest Whitaker!"

An equally obese woman dressed similarly looked at me sideways. "Forest Whitaker is a vampire?"

I pulled up the hoodie on my sweatshirt and started walking toward a private elevator between a pair of obelisks. It was in the presence of all this grandeur that I wondered if my creator felt the need to overcompensate for the fact that he'd come from nothing. Then again, maybe it was just like he'd said. He'd worked his way up from nothing and managed to achieve all of this. Maybe he just wanted to show how far he'd come.

Or maybe he just liked faux Egyptian crap.

Reaching the elevator, I saw it still had the same hand scanner as before. I hesitated before putting my palm over it, then reluctantly did so. It scanned my handprint and accepted it. The doors proceeded to open to a beautiful wood-paneled elevator with a mirror in the back. My eyes caught a little gold crucifix around Melissa's neck and I was transfixed because, for a second, I thought the cross glowed.

I was about to head in when the vampire I least wanted to see in the world came up behind me. He was wearing a dark ill-fitting suit over a button-down white shirt, with a fedora improperly resting on his head. He wasn't ugly despite his slovenly appearance—a bit like Charlie Sheen before he completely lost his mind. In his mouth was a thick cigar, a mix of pot, tobacco, and fairy dust from the smell of it.

Theodore Eaton, Ashura's creation and the voivode's *bellidux*. He was the chief torturer, bully, and thug of New Detroit. In order to keep all the supernaturals in line, he was given free rein to beat, torture, or kill anyone he considered out of line. In other words, he was a rabid cop, and coming from one of Detroit's tougher neighborhoods, you could guess what I thought of rabid cops. He'd also wronged me.

Horribly.

Seeing him, my hands extended claws. "Eaton."

Melissa stared at me, perhaps sensing through our bond just how much I hated that evil, racist son of a bitch. Strangely, in that moment, I sensed just how much she hated vampires and all the ones around her. It was a hot and passionate hatred, not at all like her understated demeanor. In that moment, I saw images of her in a red cocktail dress luring vampires outside, and moments where she stabbed them through their sleeping chests with cold iron spikes before setting them on fire or dragging them out into the sun with chains. I couldn't tell if they were fantasies or reality.

But Melissa just became a lot more interesting.

"What did he do to you?" Melissa asked, having sensed more than I wanted her to.

"None of your business."

I remembered being locked away in the basement of a building scheduled for demolition, my arms and legs chained to a metal chair and every part of my body sore from where Eaton had worked me over with his men. Vampires didn't bruise easily, but he had the advantage of superhuman strength, and his men were equipped with aluminum bats.

I was newly turned back then, still flush in my belief that I was invincible and that I was the good guy. It was a stupid belief given what I'd done, but Thoth had been very persuasive about why we'd done good things building New Detroit and taking down those who stood in the way of its construction.

Eaton, wearing a leather jacket and jeans and sporting a greaser haircut for some reason, punched me across the face. "You shouldn't have interfered in your better's feeding."

"Fuck you," I said, spitting blood on the ground.

The ultimate insult among our kind.

Eaton smiled and said, "Do you even know why you're down here? Why even your creator can't protect you?"

"Don't know, don't care," I lied, wondering how I'd ended up here.

"You took what didn't belong to you. That girl belonged to an Old One."

I remembered attending one of Voivode Ashura's parties where a despicably greasy-looking Old One had tried to take one of the mortal party guest's children. I'd ushered the child back to her parents and away before telling Thoth about it. Apparently, that had pissed some people off. Now, looking at Eaton, I wanted to kill him with my bare hands.

"She was eight-years-old, you bastard," I said, staring at him.

"She would have been eighteen eventually, or not," Eaton said. "Mortals aren't important."

"Do your worst," I said, not realizing he was only getting warmed up.

Eaton laughed. "They won't let me do my worst, Negro. The voivode was clear I couldn't rape you, cut anything off, kill you, or do any permanent damage. Then I have to release you in a week. That still leaves quite a few things open. I'm going to starve you for that time and leave a little girl of that age for you."

I blinked in horror. "You son of a bitch!"

Eaton laughed. "My mother was a baroness, son. She taught me everything I know about keeping the wrong kind in their place."

It was perhaps the only mercy I had that I don't remember actually killing the little girl, whose name I discovered was Sarah. I was a rabid dog when I attacked the scared, helpless little girl Eaton had dumped where I'd been imprisoned. I'd only come to after the horrible deed had been done and her broken, black-haired, doll-like form was in my arms.

I eventually tracked down Eaton and beat the living shit out of him. I would have killed him, had tried to kill him, but I'd done such a shit job of it that he'd managed to heal in just a few nights. The perils of using guns against the undead.

That was when I saw Melissa's eyes widen and I realized she'd seen what had happened. "My God."

I closed my eyes, ashamed.

"You're not welcome here, Exile," Eaton said, his voice dripping with disdain. "You don't have your creator's protection anymore and are any vampire's meat."

He licked his lips.

"This isn't your casino," I said, struggling not to throw myself at the self-styled lawman. "You can't afford shit. You're one of the poor vampires just like the rest of us. Tell me, is it true the voivode writes you a weekly stipend and insists on having mortals manage your money because you can't be trusted with it?"

I wasn't any good at vampiredom's catty "high school with murder" bullshit, but that was how the game was played here in the Big City. You weren't supposed to rip a man's face off; you were supposed to make him want to rip yours off so he could be dragged off for punishment. Normally by someone like Eaton.

Seeing he wasn't going to get me to attack him, Eaton sneered. "I look forward to feeding you to my dogs."

"Goodbye," I said, walking into the elevator with my servant before Melissa reluctantly followed.

The doors shut on us.

CHAPTER FIVE

It was a long elevator ride to the top.

"You know, really, I think *Reality Bites* is the worst movie ever made," David said, unable to avoid making conversation for five minutes. "I mean, a bunch of whiny crybabies sit around their apartment complaining. Was that really all my teenage self wanted to do back then? I mean, get a life, guys. What were you doing in 1994?"

"I was ten," Melissa said.

"I was trying not to get shot," I said, really wishing we'd get to the penthouse already. "Why are we friends again?"

"Because I used to work here and shared the graveyard shift?" David added a little rimshot noise at the end, presumably because he thought graveyard shift was funny. It wasn't funny the first five hundred times.

"Ah, good," I said. "I was afraid it was something that had to do with your personality and I was wondering what was wrong with me."

David wasn't going to let it go, though. "Being a terminally uncool poor vampire, but we knew that."

I was cool, dammit! "Now listen here—"

"So, what's your creator like?" Melissa, thankfully, changed the subject. "Do I have to like bow or anything?"

"He'd like it," I said, staring upward at the numbers above the door. "I wouldn't recommend it."

"Thoth is the youngest of the Old Ones," David said, sounding like he was discussing a baseball card. "He's the last one to turn two hundred and it was right before the Bailout, which he helped organize. He's a former slave, mercenary, assassin, painter, philosopher, wanderer, and magician. Oh, and he also gets more—"

I stared at my servant. "What are you, part of his fan club?"

"I'm just saying we'll be family as soon as you change me," David said. "So, you know, it's good to suck up to the rich relatives. No pun intended."

"Vampires actually slurp rather than suck," I said, correcting a long-held misconception. "The heart does most of the pumping, so you really just open your mouth and let it go into your throat. The trick is to swallow it in gulps or you lose all the flavor."

Melissa looked ill. "I could have gone my whole life without knowing that."

"Actually, you probably couldn't have gone another night. It's pretty much why your hair has blood in it."

"Oh, I didn't notice."

David reached up to touch her hair, only for Melissa to slap his hand away with a bit more force than necessary.

"Damn! I think you broke my hand."

"Deal with it," I commanded. "Also, shut the hell up during this conversation and be respectful. I don't need you getting your throat torn out. Shitty servant as you may be, you are my friend and I don't want to see you killed."

David opened his mouth to reply, then closed it before adopting a respectful posture and pose, keeping his hands behind his back.

"You could do that all the time?" Melissa asked.

"Yeah," I said.

"Then why don't you?" Melissa surprised me by asking.

"Because I'm not a monster." I remembered cradling Sarah's body in my arms in the ruins of the basement, screaming as I woke from the horrifying hunger that had destroyed my sanity and left me unable to do anything but feed. "Not much of one."

The doors opened then to the middle of Thoth's penthouse. I found myself surrounded immediately by an office that had fountain walls over black obsidian on both sides of the room, reflective marble floors, and a large stone desk resting at the other side with a window view of the casino floor below. There were weapon and armor racks scattered about, some enchanted, some not. The room was cold and austere, and evoked the kind of ambiance a castle might have if transplanted to the modern day. The place looked less like what I'd imagine a vampire hotel owner's place to look like and more like the office of Lex Luthor.

I sensed my creator's presence in the adjoining room and looked back to Melissa. She was staring at a pair of katana mounted on the wall, ones I'd known Thoth to use. He'd actually given me an authentic one from the Nineteenth Century, which I'd frequently considered hocking to pay the bills. The problem was I suspected that would be construed as an insult, and I didn't know any place other than Ebay that wouldn't screw me out of the majority of its worth.

"You guys stay here," I said, starting toward the adjoining room. "I need to talk with him alone for a second."

Melissa, nodded, looking suspiciously back at the katana every few seconds. "Yeah, sure."

David just stood there, obedient and respectful as he'd been ordered to be.

I paused at the door before turning around. "Oh, and a couple of things on the off chance you survive the next thirty minutes."

"Off chance?" Melissa asked. "What's that?"

"Yeah, don't get into the sun. It'll kill you unless you're an Old One. Don't worry about garlic, but verbena is out. I once dated this hippie chick I went to the house of and I swear it was like being tear gassed. Stake through the heart will immobilize you but not kill you, but it doesn't need to be wood, which sadly means bullets can do the trick if they don't pass through you. I once had to have four surgeries to get me back up. Fire, holy items, decapitation, monster claws or teeth, and magic can also put you in the ground for good." There were a lot of annoying little weaknesses too, like the counting thing, but was I embarrassed to share that. It was also unlikely to come up on her first night of unlife.

"Magic going to be a problem?" Melissa asked.

"If it can kill Superman, it can kill a vampire," I said, shrugging. "Something tells me you already know a lot of this, though."

Melissa didn't answer that.

I didn't know for sure she was a former vampire hunter, but those images I'd picked from her brain had been pretty intense, as had been the mention of her protest. If she was, though, then she'd probably be in the Vampire Nation's database. For obvious reasons, they kept a "Van Helsing Watch List," which was constantly updated in order to make sure they knew who to watch out for and why. I didn't blame her for wanting to kill vampires. It's what I wanted to at various times as a human. But you couldn't choose your family, and I was on Team Bloodsucker now for better or worse.

Walking through the door, I thought about how things had changed. Laws protected us now against humans, badly or not, and things were getting better. Vampires were people too now that we were allowed to be out in the open and live among regular humans. Hell, we were practically normal now.

That was when I saw, on the other side of the door, a huge, richly-decorated, candlelit bedroom. On one end was an "emperor-sized" bed with two fabulously beautiful vampire women lying on it, one black and one white, posing for Thoth as he painted a portrait of them. There were seven partially-drained naked models and two A-list celebrities spread around the bed too, their faces contorted in blissful senselessness.

"Practically normal to Vampire Wilt Chamberlain," I muttered, looking away and covering the side of my face with my hand. "Hell, Thoth, can you be less of a vampire stereotype? Some of us are trying not to live the undead Puff Daddy thing."

Thoth, shirtless and wearing a pair of silk boxers, held a palette as he stood before a terrible portrait of his surroundings. All of the people and objects looked like they'd been turned into squares before being cut up. He didn't bother to turn to me or even acknowledge my presence, which I found to be insulting.

"Ah, hello, Peter," the white girl on the bed said. She had short red hair and a body I was doing my best not to look at, but was of a classic shape, not too thin or too large, which sculptors would have loved to make.

I almost fled out the door as I realized who it was. "Voivode Ashura. Doing some, uh, modeling I see?"

Ashura was a four-hundred-year-old Turkish vampire raised as a slave in an Ottoman sultan's harem. Somehow, she'd caught the attention of an Old One and had been raised on the politics of the Vampire Nation ever since. I should have thought harder about the fact that Eaton had been downstairs. The voivode's favorite lackey was never too far from her side, and she was prone to using the

Apophis as her place of business, other vampires' territory or not.

"Indeed, I am," Ashura said, stretching her arms and causing Thoth to pull back from his canvas. "I believe you're familiar with my associate Fatima?"

I didn't look at her, but the only Fatima I knew was Fatima al Ali, a killer of men who abused slave women during the time leading up to the Civil War. Her Muslim name wasn't her original one, but she'd taken on a new one, as many vampires did. Thoth had brought her over and trained her to be a weapon against his enemies. They were lovers too, though that wasn't exactly uncommon among the Old Ones, as they seemed to consider sex to be slightly more personal than a handshake. Last I heard she was working as a Magister for the Council of Ancients.

If she was here, someone was going to die.

Maybe me.

Crap.

Calm yourself, Thoth's voice spoke in my mind. *Fatimah and Ashura are just here to discuss an upcoming conference of Vampire Nation leaders we're hosting this weekend. Also, to have their portraits done.*

Oh, I said, ignoring the fact my creator was reading my thoughts again. *That's all?*

Well, we're all going to have sex afterward, like we did before with those mortals, but that's the lifestyle you think is so stereotypical.

Ha ha.

We're vampires, Peter. I have no desire to lose our culture of sex, excess, wealth, and art for the mundanity of a human, monogamous, two-partner, white-picket-fence suburban hell. You'll come to appreciate it once you've made your fortune.

Yeah, still working on that. I wished I could take a deep listen. Listen, I've got a serious problem—

Thoth interrupted me. *Yes, I've already read it from your mind.*

Thoth looked up from his painting. "Your Majesty, I should point out that one of my creations from Atlanta will be visiting the city. Her name is Melissa Morris and she's been working for me undercover."

I looked over at the two women, keeping them at eye level to gauge their reaction.

"Oh?" Ashura asked, shrugging her dainty shoulders. "Why have I not been informed of her before?"

Fatima raised an eyebrow but didn't make a comment, undoubtedly knowing her creator had never created another vampire other than me.

"You never asked," Thoth said, amused. "I, of course, will pay the tithe for her stay and make sure she obeys all the laws of the city."

"I haven't agreed to her staying yet," Ashura said, her eyes briefly flashing red. It looked like she was going to tear someone's throat out. It was amazing how she could go from coquettish to terrifying in an instant.

Thoth bowed his head. "I, of course, will send her away if you so desire."

Ashura was silent for a moment, then said, "Anything she does is on your head, Thoth. You and your child's. Remember that."

"Of course."

"I have lost my appetite for modeling. Leave it for when I return. Oh, and get a better quality of celebrity next time. More Hepburn and less flavor of the month." Ashura proceeded to get up and throw on a robe before picking up a thousand- dollar dress off the ground, then casually walking to a secondary elevator built in the back of the room.

Her disappearance from the room seemed to remove a considerable air of menace.

Thoth glared at me. "Thank you so very much for dropping that in my lap."

"Where else is he going to turn, T?" Fatima asked, getting off the bed. "You banished him from your inner circle's territory, which includes much of his hometown. You should be grateful he trusts you enough to come to him."

I wasn't exactly happy about Fatima coming to my defense. I was a grown-ass man who could do his own fighting. That was one of the big things I hated about vampire society. In addition to all of the wealth being concentrated in the hands of a lucky few Old Ones, everyone was also so damned condescending even when they were trying to be nice.

"How much trouble are you in right now?" I asked, grimacing and accidentally cutting my lip with fang. I hated when shit like that happened.

"It depends on how much she knows," Thoth said. "But given she casually reads the minds of other vampires the way I do my children's, I expect everything. Ashura just can't prove it."

"Oh," I said, taking a deep breath. "Thanks."

Thoth walked up to me and put his arm on my shoulder. "You are my creation, even though I expected much more from you by now."

"Thanks, Dad, I really need all the verbal abuse I lost out on when my human father abandoned me."

Fatima laughed.

Even Thoth smirked, then swiftly lost his cheerful expression. "You realize you've brought a vampire hunter into our midst."

That just confirmed what I'd suspected, but it was still disappointing. "Is it proven she's a hunter?"

Fatima threw on her own black robe. "Thoth contacted me with the name. She *is* on the VHWL. Seven confirmed vampires killed and an unknown number of other supernaturals, but no more than ten. Interestingly, of all the vampire kills, six of them were confirmed to be murderers of the innocent."

In my experience, that was like saying six of them were confirmed to drink water. "So, what are you saying, she only hunted guilty vampires? What about the seventh?"

"He was found guilty of rape," Thoth said. "The seventeen-year-old girl later recanted her testimony, but only after Ms. Morris killed him."

I processed that. "So, what does this all mean?"

Thoth's tone became grave. "David told me something intriguing."

"That's a first," I said.

"When the emperor has no clothes, only the fool dares mention it," Thoth said. "He said this woman can speak the name of the Nazarene and other holy figures without pain. That she can actually wear a cross around her neck without harm."

"Is that important?" I asked.

Thoth nodded. "It means I may know the name of her sire. If I'm right, then it's very likely he's come to kill us all."

I absorbed his words, taking note of the fact Thoth never engaged in hyperbole. "Man, do you ever have any good news?"

"Not if I want to tell the truth," Thoth said.

"When has that has ever stopped you before?" I asked, joking.

Thoth frowned.

Fatima said. "We need you to seduce this girl and get her to lead you to Renaud."

I nodded along, then did a double take. "Wait, what?"

CHAPTER SIX

"You want me to what now?" I asked, not sure if I'd heard that correctly.

"Seduce her," Thoth said, as if it were the most normal request in the world.

"Is that going to be a problem?" Fatimah said. "Does she not prefer men? Even then, with the power you should be able—"

"Please don't finish that sentence," I said, raising my hands. "I don't know if you've noticed but I'm not a very seductive guy. I work at a fucking convenience store."

Thoth frowned. "You're a vampire, Peter, a primal force of sexuality and power before which all mortals are inclined to bow down. Princesses, duchesses, and queens have begged me to drink their blood."

"Kings too," Fatimah said, reaching over to rub my chest with her fingertip. "Although I prefer an earthier sort."

"Guys, don't make this weird. Well, *weirder*," I said, looking between them. "I think you really overestimate the appeal of the undead these days. I mean, have you been on 16th Street? Some of the homeliest undead you've ever seen. Not even hookers will take them."

"It's what you get when everyone knows about vampires," Fatimah said. "You create just one wrong person and then their friends are created who create their friends and so on."

I really hoped I never became as classist (speciesist?) as these two. "Not to put too fine a point on it, but did you also miss she's a frigging vampire hunter? I don't think she's going to want to get down with the kind of guy she was raised to fight."

Fatimah snorted. "I've slept with six. Some of which I let live."

"There is a fine line between love and hate," Thoth said. "Plus, she's in a vulnerable state now and you're a sympathetic ear. She also drank your blood during her transformation, so you should be able to influence her, as Fatimah was alluding to."

I sighed. "How about I *not* get all mind-rapey? Okay?"

Thoth sighed. "You were the best servant I ever had. Fine, do this your way. We need to find Renaud, no matter the cost."

"That's the second time you've mentioned this guy. Who is he?" I asked, wondering just how deep of a pile of shit I'd fallen into.

Very deep, Thoth said in my head before speaking aloud. "Renaud de Bures is the hunter who hunts the hunters. He is an Old One, a former Knight Templar who was scheduled to be burned at the stake with Jacques de Molay in 1314. You are familiar with the Knights Templar?"

"I watch the History Channel," I explained. "Big Bad Crusaders, killed a lot of Muslims, became bankers, got killed by a French king who wanted their money. Subject of a lot of Dan Brown novels."

"More or less the sum of it," Thoth said, pulling on a pair of leather pants and putting on a silk shirt, which made him look like a Black, bald Lestat. "His creator, an unknown woman who may have been our founder Lamia, proceeded to change him in the dungeons of Philip the Fourth. Christoph was unusual as a churchman in that time, as he actually believed in God and took his transformation poorly. He travelled to Jerusalem to beseech his God for the power to destroy all vampires."

"Must have been disappointed when the Big G didn't answer."

"Something did, actually," Thoth said, his voice sounding haunted.

I blinked. "Excuse me?"

"There are many things beyond this Earth. Things that make even the Ancient Ones wary," Thoth said, frowning. "*Whatever* he spoke with, Renaud emerged from Jerusalem with the power to kill Old Ones and an unquenchable thirst for the blood of those he deemed to be sinners. He was immune to the traditional weaknesses of vampire kind and possessed an ivory curved blade capable of stealing the power of other vampires."

"So he's an evil version of Connor MacLeod?" I asked, trying to process that there was a seven-hundred-year-old religious fanatic

Old One running around killing vampires. That seemed to me to be the kind of thing you'd tell newborns.

Thoth and Fatima stared.

"Right, you probably never saw *Highlander*. You poor bastards," I muttered, embarrassed by my statement. "Can't this guy have just lived to be two hundred years old, become an Old One, and develop the psychic powers to do that naturally?"

"That's what I believe," Fatimah said. "Still, he has a mystique, and even the Council of Ancients is terrified of him. The fact that his creations are all immune to religious symbols helps us track them. That's part of the reason I was in the area, tracking down the trail of newborn vampires he's left behind."

"Wait, guy who wants to kill all vampires makes other vampires?" I said, trying to keep up with this.

Thoth nodded. "He's made thousands. One of the easiest ways to make a massive witch hunt against the undead is to create lots of vampires, let them turn into draugr, and unleash them on the public. It's triggered mass hysteria and persecutions and killed countless innocents. I don't really care about human life all that much, but he even sickens me. There is no greater doer of evil than the one who believes he is doing it for a noble purpose."

That was sobering. "Are you sure he's the guy who made Melissa?"

"Melissa, now is it?" Thoth said. "No, I'm not. But Renaud has been sighted in the New Detroit area. It represents everything he despises most: human acceptance of the undead and a turning away from superstition-driven fear of the other."

I frowned, not liking his attitude. "If you don't care about human life, why do you give a shit about Detroit?"

Thoth shrugged. "They might become a more interesting species in a few centuries. Besides, we come from them. Humans also sometimes create someone truly exceptional, and we can make another one of our race. Besides, as the people on the ground can attest, they have their amusements."

"Yeah, right," I said, realizing this conversation wasn't going anywhere good. Thoth had once been a lot more forgiving of the human race. I wondered if he'd changed his opinion on mankind or if he'd just stopped lying to me. "All right, I'll see if I can get the information out of her."

"Good man," Thoth said, heading to the door.

"What's going to happen to if we do find and kill this Big Badass Vampiric Vampire Hunter?

Thoth looked back. "What do you *think*?"

That wasn't good. Not entirely unexpected, but not good. I hadn't exactly bonded with Melissa over the course of our three hours of acquaintance, but I wasn't eager to see her killed either. Maybe it was the fact that she'd feasted on my blood, and I could sense her fear and uncertainty, sense that her entire worldview was crumbling. Indeed, reaching out, I sensed ...

Rage.

Betrayal.

Murderous intent.

Oh shit.

Thoth opened the door, only to have a steel bolt bury itself in his shoulder. The bolt was covered in blood runes that caused him to fall to one knee. I could feel the power of the runes from where I stood. On the other side of the door, I saw Melissa holding a crossbow in hand while David was on the ground, clutching his stomach.

"You're not putting me down!" Melissa hissed, baring her fangs.

Enhanced hearing must be one of her gifts. "See, this is why you don't keep a bunch of antique weapons on your wall."

Fatimah, however, wasn't listening, as she was too furious at Thoth's injury. Turning into a literal shadow, she flickered across the room and was suddenly behind Melissa. That was when Melissa lifted the crossbow and attempted to use it as a cross to hold her at bay. Fatimah actually took a step back before smashing it to pieces with a single blow of her fist. The assassin then grabbed Melissa in a headlock and bared her fangs to rip out her throat.

"Stop!" I said, surprising myself by stepping forward with my hands raised. "Thoth isn't dead. We also need her to find this crazy murder hobo vampire you're looking for."

Fatimah didn't put away her fangs. "She's a murderer of our kind."

Melissa struggled in Fatimah's grip but didn't seem to make any progress. I could see why when I looked and saw that Fatimah's shadow had reached up to grab her by the legs and was holding her in place.

Freaky.

"Maybe it's time we proved we're not the monsters she thought we were," I said, feeling like an idiot for appealing to a vampire's sense of morality. Still, I didn't have any other ideas about how to get her to stop. "Besides, she's our kind now."

Surprisingly, Fatimah finally put away her fangs. "Order her not to do us any further harm and I won't kill her."

"I don't think—" I started to say.

Fatimah's eyes silenced all dissent.

"Right," I corrected myself. "Melissa, I command you not to try and murder these people who could rip you to pieces with their eyes closed. Also to get a better attitude, because I just went to pretty elaborate lengths to try to help your ass, while you were part of a group that would set me on fire."

This actually seemed to have an effect on Melissa. She started to calm down and stopped struggling, looking confused now more than anything. It seemed that her feeding on my blood during her transformation really had given me power over her.

Perhaps as much as her creator.

"Ask her who her creator is," Fatimah said.

"She doesn't remember," I insisted.

"Make her!" Fatimah's voice let me know she was only seconds from ripping her head off.

"I'll check her mind," I said, not sure how to do that but hoping I could wing it on pure instinct.

Putting my hand out toward Melissa and bracing myself against the floor, I contemplated the images I'd picked up from Melissa's mind before on the casino floor and—this sounded dirty even to me—attempted to probe her.

Older vampires could learn your entire life story and your ATM card number from a causal glance, but I wasn't exactly talented at this. Four years of vampirism had consisted primarily of living off summoned animals and working a steady series of dead-end jobs that seemed to get progressively worse rather than better.

Entering into Melissa's mind, I found myself surrounded by images I couldn't really sort through. My blood was serving as a sort of anchor for my presence, and it was infused into her very bones even as it had merged with the blood of her creator. Trying to concentrate on the images I'd seen, I was only deluged by more.

A baby sister.

A bloody car wreck.

Training with swords.

Training with guns.

Training with explosives.

Damn.

As I waded through her memories and thoughts, I found myself banging up against some sort of wall, which I recognized as the kind of barrier other vampires erected around the memories of mortals and sometimes other supernaturals. I'd never heard of it being used against another vampire, though. It should have been impossible. Reluctantly, I focused on my bond with Melissa and pushed forward.

"Ah!" Melissa cried out, the look on her face one of pure agony.

"Sorry, girl."

Fear.

Anxiety.

Pain.

Confusion.

Running away in terror.

I saw a tall Nordic-looking man with black hair, a goatee, a ponytail, muscles covering his body from head to toe, and fangs. He was dressed in a brown trench coat, black turtleneck sweater, and blue jeans, with a sword on his back.

Fangs.

His fangs.

"Does Renaud look like a Caucasian mullet-wearing Dwayne Johnson?" I paused, not really expecting an answer.

"Yes," Thoth said, surprising me by getting up and pulling the crossbow bolt out of his shoulder. It had just barely missed his heart, which was good shooting given the second she'd had to aim. "I see the image in your mind, Peter, and that's Renaud all right."

"Great," I muttered, knowing that had virtually guaranteed her a death sentence. Not that she had much chance after trying to kill Thoth.

That was when my probing of Melissa's mind revealed something else. A more complete memory of what had been blocked appeared in my head. It was a weird sensation remembering yourself as someone else, especially another sex, but in that moment I *was* Melissa.

I remembered driving down the back roads around New Detroit in a 2016 SUV that had been bought by the Human Rights League for her with the tithes of members. Melissa had always felt a little guilty about the lavish spending of the group on its agents, but right now was just grateful to have transportation she could take. Her thoughts were muddled and I couldn't quite follow them as she pulled into the Qwik & Shop to use the bathroom. One thing I knew, though—she was desperate and terrified.

I—well, Melissa—remembered washing my hands before turning around and seeing Renaud in the room. He wasn't immediately going for my throat, though, and it stunned me, Peter, to realize that I, Melissa, knew him. OK, this whole flashback/mind-joining thing was really starting to mess with my sense of reality.

Melissa knew him.

She pulled out her cross necklace. "Stay back, monster."

Renaud shook his head, stepping forward. His voice was a thick baritone with the generic European accent many older vampires tended to adopt when speaking English. "I thought we were past this, my beloved. Even if I was not blessed by God with immunity to his touch, I am too old for this to have an effect. Besides, why would you turn a cross to me?"

Melissa remembered several passionate nights with him.

Oh hell no!

Ugh!

I almost broke my connection right there.

Melissa, however, remained resolved. "That was before I realized what kind of person you are. What you're planning to do in New Detroit."

Renaud's expression darkened. "New Detroit is an embodiment of everything vile and corrupt in the Modern World. It is a pure expression of the crass materialism and godlessness into which your civilization has allowed itself to fall. The perversities and degeneracies may climax in the acceptance of vampires, but it has many other villainies that make it worthy of destruction."

"You intend to blow up a casino," Melissa said. "Kill hundreds of people."

"No." Renaud shook his head. "Thousands."

Melissa took a step back.

Renaud transfixed her with his gaze. "If you would betray the cause, dearest flower, then I fear your soul is already lost. I would give you a quick death, but I cannot allow the possibility that necromancers would extract your secrets. Better still you'd be among the damned who will be caught in the crossfire when humanity realizes what horrors they have let through their door."

He erased her memory.

Then drank her dry.

Forcibly.

Savoring every bit of her fear as he took sexual delight, fondling her and forcing her to feel joy even as he killed her.

Then rebirthed her.

Shit.

Our link broke and my head pounded. It was the first headache I'd had since my transformation. Well, not hunger-related, at least.

"Damn, girl," I said, shaking my head. "That's some fucked-up shit."

Melissa looked up, a terrified expression on her face. "You need to get your security down to the parking garage immediately."

"Why?" Fatimah asked.

"I didn't remember why I was here until now. I was coming to warn you." Melissa's expression was horrified. "The casino Renaud is going to blow up is the Apophis. He's using the Human Rights League to do it."

CHAPTER SEVEN

I remember a day when my father had been counting on a payoff from an investment that had involved a lot of shady white-collar stuff. He'd thought he was the con man rather than the mark. Thoth's reaction reminded me of his when he found out the truth.

"Gods damned, son of a bitch!" Thoth shouted, going to his desk and then slamming his fists down on the top of it.

Cracking the stone.

"Damn," I said, staring at him. "Why can't I do that?"

Thoth wasn't finished, though. "This is what I get for trying to build an accord with the humans. All they can do is eat, breed, kill, and die. They can't bring themselves to imagine a life better than their plebeian dull little lives unless it's force fed to them by Fox News or reality TV! When someone tries to show them a better way, do you know what they do? They lash out! Even if it means their destruction! Damn them and damn the horse their pee-brained monkey-brained bodies rode in on."

"Okay," I lifted my hands, trying to calm him down. "That was *enormously* racist."

This was an ugly side to my creator and one I was increasing starting to believe was recent rather than something he'd been hiding. Since I'd become a vampire, New Detroit had expanded and done wonders for human-undead relations, but I wasn't so sure he could see that.

I couldn't imagine what it had to be like for the guy at the top dealing with all of the trials and tribulations to keep it all running, especially since so many bigots were determined to tear it all down. It made me almost sympathetic enough to forget how many bodies he'd had to bury, figurative and literal, to get where he was.

Thoth growled. "Human aren't a race! They're a disease. A disease the gods have decided to curse vampires to be unable to live without."

"Channeling a little Agent Smith there, T, and it's not a good look for you," I said, shaking my head. "Besides, it's a vampire who is behind this."

"If the Human Rights League does any damage to my casino, I'm going to hunt down every single member of that insipid organization and feed them to hellhounds."

"That's a fair cop," I said, admitting I'd probably be reacting every bit as badly if they were messing with my people. "The thing is, we have to find out when they're going to make their strike at us and stop it."

Thoth looked up. "Really, Peter, I hadn't guessed. What's next, telling me we're going to have to kill Renaud? Avoid verbena and crosses? Drink blood every night?"

"No need to be sarcastic."

"There's *always* a need to be sarcastic." Thoth snorted as he turned to the laptop on his desk and started typing away on it.

Fatimah, surprisingly, released Melissa and then helped David to his feet. My servant was a bit dazed and confused, but that was his normal state so I wasn't too concerned. The fact that he politely thanked Fatimah and dusted himself off told me I needed to remove my order for him to be quiet and respectful, though.

In an hour or two.

"Do you know when they're supposed to detonate this bomb?" Fatimah asked, now much more conciliatory to Melissa.

Melissa shook her head. "I only know Renaud managed to convince the other heads of the HRL to assist in the project, and they were going to strike soon. They locked me out of the loop when they realized I not only wasn't interested in going along with their plan but wanted to actively stop them."

"And yet you still were banging Osama Bin Knightly," I said, not believing she'd been involved with that guy.

Melissa looked at me in contempt. I'd clearly struck a nerve, but I felt ashamed for throwing that at her. It was none of my business whom she slept with.

Even if they were terrorists.

"That is a terrible insult," David said, finally speaking. "I mean, it doesn't even make any sense."

"How are you speaking? I ordered you to shut up," I said, upset.

David shrugged his shoulders. "It wore off."

"I hate being the low man on the vampire totem pole," I hissed, clenching my fangs. "It's like Basic Training all over again."

"They're here," Thoth said, still staring at his computer.

"What?" I said, walking over to Thoth's desk and looking over his shoulder.

Thoth had tapped into the security feeds of the Apophis's expansive security system, and I got a sight of the bottom level of the underground parking garage. There were a half-dozen white Blood & Wine delivery vans down below with armed men moving between them. A facial recognition scanner was pulling up each of their identities, and it was one HRL nutbag after another.

"Shouldn't your security guys have picked up on this?" I asked, watching the HRL terrorists unload a couple of staked vampires from the backs of their trucks.

"Yes, they should have," Thoth said, growling. "These are my secondary hidden cameras away from the main ones, though. They've compromised the original ones. They're running a loop of earlier footage."

Melissa closed her eyes, looking guilt-stricken. "They intend to blow up the place and make it look like a feud between Old Ones. They hope it'll turn people against the Vampire Nation and get all of your special rights repealed."

"Which will rapidly result in thousands of vampire deaths," Thoth said, continuing to look at the security footage. "Ingenious."

"Shouldn't you be evacuating the casino?" I asked, frowning. "What with the whole 'terrorists in the basement' thing?"

Thoth looked up to Fatimah. "Get a show going outside the building. Have someone shapeshift into Freddie Mercury or something. Offer it free and get as many people as possible away from the probable blast radius."

Fatimah frowned. "I'd prefer to deal with those fools downstairs, but I will do as you command. Come with me, slave."

"Do you mean me?" David asked.

Fatimah glared, then walked to the elevator.

"Yes, ma'am," David squeaked before following her.

"Freddie Mercury's been dead since '91," I said.

"That's what most people think," Thoth said, rising from his desk. "We can't risk people believing the Apophis and New Detroit are vulnerable to terrorism."

"People's lives are at stake!" Melissa said, regardless of the hypocrisy.

"So is this city," Thoth said, staring at her. "The only reason people aren't all dragging vampires out into the sun or dousing us with gasoline like your group wants to do is because of a concentrated hundred-and-ten-year plan to make us palatable to mankind. From Bram Stoker to that Meyer woman, we have been subtly brainwashing humanity into believing our race could live in peace with yours. New Detroit is symbolic of that, and if it fails, then all of that will be for nothing."

"Getting some mixed signals here, chief," I said, not at all happy with his decision. "Are you for or against humans?"

Thoth frowned. "Sometimes I wonder that myself. Peter, I need your help."

"That must have hurt for you to ask."

"More than you know. I released you from my service when I made you, but it was your choice to abandon New Detroit."

Thoth tapped a button on the side of his desk and a hidden compartment revealed itself on the wall containing not medieval weapons like crossbows or swords, but Uzis, shotguns, pistols, and even a bandolier of grenades.

"You banished me."

"Temporarily. I was protecting you," Thoth said. "If it didn't look like I was punishing you for what you did, they would have come down on you harder."

I clenched my fists. "You know what Eaton did to me. He deserved to die."

"He will," Thoth said. "But one must be patient with one's enemies."

"Screw patience."

Melissa cleared her throat. "Uh, guys?"

I had actually forgotten about her. "Oh, hey, yeah! Uh, this is awkward, but we're going to go murder a bunch of your people now."

Melissa blinked at the casualness of my statement and I wondered about that myself. Tonight was bringing out my inner psychopath.

"Can't you guys just call the police?" Melissa asked. "I mean, you own them here, right?"

Thoth gave a half-snort. "It runs into the same problem as evacuating the building. Besides, even rich vampires are still vampires to the authorities. No, better to handle this in-house."

"Besides, aren't you being a wee bit hypocritical?" I asked, going over to the rack and weapons to choose. "Why didn't you call the police, FBI, or the Department of Supernatural Security?"

Melissa fidgeted a bit. "I didn't think you'd believe me. The Human Rights League has called in fake bomb threats to hurt supernatural businesses before."

I shook my head. "Real piece of work you are, lady."

Thoth got up from his seat. "We still have a few minutes from the looks of things. We need to kill every single one of these bastards."

"Fatimah would be great for that," I said, picking up a TriStar Cobra Mag Pump, the bandolier of grenades, plus two pistols I holstered at my side. "But I'm good."

Thoth, meanwhile, got himself an M16 covered in blood runes. "I'd rather have Fatimah down there by my side as well, but if we're killed there, I'd like for my lineage to survive."

Nice to know I was the Jan Brady to Fatimah's Marcia. "I thought you couldn't be killed as an Old One."

"If I'm blown up and buried under however many tons of rocks, I might eventually regenerate after a few centuries, but I won't necessarily be myself anymore. More likely it'll be a monster akin to a draugr, only a hundred times more powerful."

"You are always just a ray of sunshine," I said. "By which I mean a guy who burns my ass."

"It's also possible Renaud may be down there," Thoth said, loading his weapon before heading to the door, passing by Melissa without acknowledgement. Once both of us left, she'd be effectively trapped up here until someone came up to get her. I could also probably order her to stay.

"What happens then?" I asked, following him. "Assuming Tall, Dark, and Crazy is down there."

"We die."

Screw Thoth being a ray of sunshine. He was the whole frigging sun. "I'll bear that in mind."

Thoth summoned the elevator. "Thank you for doing this, Peter."

"Don't mention it," I said. "I mean that."

"I want to help," Melissa suddenly piped up.

I almost laughed. "Lady, you must be out of your damned mind if you think we're going to let you anywhere near the group downstairs."

"I can fight," Melissa said. "Probably better than you."

"Tell that to Uday Hussein and his werejackal bodyguards," I said. "Besides, why do you want to kill these people? They're your crew."

"They're not my crew," Melissa said, her voice lowering and becoming almost a hiss. "They sacrificed anything resembling the moral high ground when they decided to involve innocents in this."

"Versus vampires," I said, not intending to let her off the hook for being a hunter.

"I'm revaluating some of my beliefs," Melissa said, not caring about how she was coming off. "Even so, I'd already come to believe only most vampires were evil while alive."

"Most vampires?" I asked.

"Most," Melissa repeated, unrepentant.

The problem with what she was saying was, well, it was true. We were a race of complete assholes. That was the difference, I suppose, between bigotry against the undead and bigotry against most minority groups.

We were getting better, though.

"Thoth?" I turned to him as the elevator doors opened in front of us. I didn't actually want her with us, but it occurred to me it was better to keep her close. Maybe it would cause the other bastards to hesitate, and I didn't want her left alone here with all of these weapons and figuring a way out of the penthouse.

"She's your responsibility now," Thoth said. "If she misbehaves, just order her to kill herself."

"Ha ha," I said, rolling my eyes. "You go get a weapon off the rack then, Melissa. Quickly. If you're willing to kill these anti-bloodsucker terrorists, then more power to you."

I added a little oomph to my words to make them a subtle

command. I was getting the hang of this mind-control crap.

"Thank you." Melissa grabbed a katana off the wall then zipped across the room into the elevator ahead of us. She took up residence in the back and the two of us were forced to get in front of her with our backs to her.

Point to her.

The three of us waited inside the cramped confines of the elevator as the doors shut and it started to head down toward the parking garage.

"Nice job with the speed," I said. "You hit the superpower jackpot, it seems."

"I can't do much," Melissa said. "What I've done just came naturally."

"Super-speed, super-hearing, and an immunity to holy stuff," I said, looking at the doors. "That's more than I could do for months. Hell, I'm still just the undead Doctor Doolittle and floaty guy. I may be able to kick a little more ass than usual, but some vamps have all the luck."

"I can sense you have not come into your full potential and whatever latent gifts you still possess will be exceptional when they manifest." Thoth surprised me by taking a reassuring tone. "Assuming you survive long enough for them to."

"Ah, that's the Thoth I know. Encouraging yet condescending."

"I try," Thoth said.

I couldn't say I wasn't nervous. It had been a long time since I'd been involved in one of these little blood feuds. I'd busted a lot of heads in my service to Thoth, and that had been only the tip of the iceberg. It seemed every single vampire who wasn't getting part of the New Detroit project had a chip on his shoulder about Thoth, and all of them seemed to want to take it out on me. In a way I was glad to have been banished from New Detroit after the incident with Eaton. I just wish it hadn't been quite so far.

I paused, remembering an early part of my conversation with Baron. "Wait a damn minute. You can order me to kill myself?"

"No, of course not," Thoth said. "Your will is much too powerful."

I looked at him intently. "Are you just saying that?"

"Would it make a difference if I said my master could have done the same thing to me?"

"And where's he?" I asked.

"Dead," Thoth said.

"Then no."

"The price of immortality, Peter," Thoth said, staring intently at the doors. It was his "I'm going to murder some fuckers" face, and I'd seen him put it on only a few times before. Usually before, well, the aforementioned murdering some fuckers.

"Yeah, but that's the thing about vampire immortality. You have to be dead to get it."

"Funny," Melissa said from behind us.

I actually wasn't joking, as it seemed like every poor bastard I'd seen made in the past four years was more likely to get killed in their first few years than to go on to become an Old One. Vampires would overwhelm the world if they didn't live lives of constant violence. Thoth wanted to make it so vampires could live in peace, dislike or distaste for humanity aside, but I wasn't sure the opposition was wrong. We were monsters. It was better there were only a few of us.

A few seconds later, the doors of the elevator opened to the parking garage. It was the bottom level and there were only a few cars down there, most of which belonging to the Blood and Wine delivery service. The elevator to the penthouse was disguised so it shouldn't have tipped off the hunters. Instead, though, they were waiting for us.

Roughly half the hunters were dressed in white delivery personal attire but not doing a very good job of hiding their military bearing and body armor underneath. The others didn't even do that much, with attire resembling Eaton's Matrix thugs.

They had assault rifles, grenade launchers, a couple of flame-throwers, and a few silver machetes. The latter confused me until I realized this group probably killed shapeshifters too. That wasn't always a given with hunters and some of them actually *were* werecreatures of various sorts.

One of them was holding an Alcotán-100 anti-tank rocket launcher, which he was pointing right at us. He'd been waiting for us or, at least, had been prepared to shoot at anyone who came through the disguised elevator.

"Shit," I said.

Right before the hunter fired a rocket at us.

CHAPTER EIGHT

They say your life flashes before you when you're about to die, and in this case, it was literally true. Time seemed to slow down, and as the Alcotán-100's rocket came toward me at a glacial place, I remembered the moment that had led me to this place.

My banishment.

I was huddled in the corner in the corner of the burnt-out building I'd been living in for the past week. It was in Old Detroit, one of the many places condemned for the final stage of the New Detroit project. There was a dead cat beside me and a bunch of rats, but I was still starving for blood. Starving but repulsed by it. Imagine that, a vampire repulsed by blood. All it took was a little girl dying.

"I'm sorry about what happened," Thoth said, standing over me in a trench coat covering an expensive green business suit with an ankh on his lapel. He stood out like a diamond among coal in this hellhole, but I wished he'd go away. He hadn't done anything to help me when I'd needed him and as far as I was concerned, he was just another selfish egotistical Old One out for himself.

"Screw you," I said, feeling the shakes.

The Need was upon me.

"You can't live off animal blood, Peter," Thoth said, looking like he was trying to be sympathetic but literally having forgotten how. "You'll eventually starve to death, go mad, and become a draugr. Then whatever you're feeling now will only be magnified by whatever you do until you're satisfied."

"I'm not drinking from people again," I said, feeling less than confident in my lie. Last night, desperate to have the taste of human blood again, I'd started feeding on the homeless around the building.

As if they didn't have enough problems.

Thoth, thankfully, didn't call me on it. "They're hunting for you now. The other vampires of the city, I mean. The only reason I got to you first is because one of the knights had a considerable number of markers at the Apophis."

"They're hunting *me*? For tearing Eaton's throat out?" I said, unable to believe even Vampire Nation could be so cruel.

"Yes."

I still remembered coming at Eaton while he'd been sitting down at a strip club to eat a roofied sixteen-year-old girl. I'd killed his two bodyguards and laid into him with my shotgun before coming at him with claws and fangs. He'd looked like Jason Voorhees had taken a machete to him a hundred times by the end.

"Worth it. I'm glad I killed the child-killing bastard." I spit out a bit of rat fur stuck in my teeth. Destroying Eaton helped me cope with the fact that I was his weapon for murdering a child. That I was a child-killing bastard too.

"He's not dead," Thoth said, his expression sour. "It might have been better if you had killed him, but he will recover from the wounds you inflicted on him."

"Fuck," I muttered, disbelieving. How the hell had he survived the beating and slashing I gave him? What did it take to kill one of our kind? "He deserves to die."

"Yes," Thoth said. "He does. You need to—"

"I can still taste her!" I said, bolting from the ground and grabbing him by the shoulders. "I still remember what it felt like to drink her blood, to feel her life run down my throat, and it was wonderful! What the hell did you make me!"

That was when Thoth broke my jaw with one blow, sending me spiraling down to the ground. "Cease this whining 'Louis, Nick Knight, *Being Human*' bullshit! You are a vampire! We do not engage in self-pity."

I was so dazed by the blow that it took me a second to register anything more than the fact that my creator watched *Being Human*. "You don't know what it's like."

Thoth's gaze was penetrating. "*Of course* I know what it's like. *Every* vampire knows what it's like to kill an innocent and hate yourself for it. My own creator, Doubye, made sure I was good and insane with hunger before unleashing me on my family. My crime? Maintaining contact with them post-death."

The full implications of that hit me. "He could have just ordered you to avoid them."

"Yes, he could have," Thoth said, a guttural growl escaping his lips. "He wanted me to divorce myself from the living world in a way that was irreparable."

"It worked," I said, feeling my jaw heal. It made me hungry again. "You're not remotely human."

"Thank you," Thoth said, not missing a beat. "Because Doubye was right, even if I hate him to this day. We can't let ourselves become too attached to mortals. For a century after my release, I spent it hunting slavers, slave traders, and those who profited from the Peculiar Institution. I exterminated hundreds."

"Can't blame you there."

Thoth sighed. "I could have used my powers to release slaves instead, to bind politicians into working against it, or to fight those undead who were using it as a means to get free meals. I only recognized it was an excuse when I slaughtered the five-year-old daughter of someone whose sole crime was being born to wealth made by evil. That's when I decided to abandon my old name and become Thoth. To reinvent myself into the man I am today. I have shed my past."

I sincerely doubted that. "So that's your advice? To forget about it? To get over it?"

"Yes. Let go of your guilt or find a way to live with it," Thoth said, sighing. "Don't allow yourself to become the monster humans wish to make you. Don't live down to their expectations or try to absorb their morality. They're not worth it."

"Easy for you to say."

Thoth closed his eyes. "Doubye's atrocities as a vampire were miniscule compared to the ones I've seen humans commit. Eaton will have his due, but only if you learn to play the game and bide your time. A vampire's vengeance is like a fine wine. It's measured in decades before it comes to maturity."

He was like a broken record there. "I can't do that."

Thoth opened his eyes and gave a sympathetic shake of his head. "I know, nor would I want you to. I embraced you because you have the stamina to make it through immortality. That you can survive and want to live despite all the horrible things you've seen and done. Because I believe in you."

"So you'll help me kill him? For good this time?" I looked up. It was the first real moment of hope I'd had in months.

"No," Thoth said, deflating me in an instant. "I need to be seen punishing you in order to separate myself during this critical juncture. I also need to deflect their desire to punish you by making it seem you're already suffering."

"Fuck you!" I hissed.

Thoth continued. "You're banished from New Detroit indefinitely. Do not return to me unless it is an emergency."

I spit a wad of bloody saliva at him, which landed on his shoes. "I'll never return to you."

"Your absence from the city until Eaton is completely healed will allow heads and blood to cool. It'll probably be safe to return in a year's time. I can't be seen to help you in any way and it won't be safe to go to any of the major U.S. cities. It's very likely the voivodes will want to curry favor with Ashura by sending you back to her. So either stay nearby in one of the adjoining towns or go to Europe." Thoth turned around to leave. "Good luck."

I didn't say anything.

On his way out, he pulled a blood bag from his suit's interior and placed it on the ground. AB positive. My favorite. I drank it after he left like it was the sweetest thing ever. In the end, time cooled the anger I felt toward him and I was actually glad we were going out like this.

Reconciled.

That was when I realized the rocket was still coming toward us and I wasn't just having a flashback, I was actually physically seeing everything moving around me in slow motion. It was some serious bullet time shit and I actually froze because it was such a surreal sight.

"Get out of the way!" Melissa suddenly shouted, breaking me from my stasis. She grabbed me and proceeded to move me at heightened speed, even in the comparative world of slow motion around us, out of the way, while Thoth moved himself from the elevator and around the concrete blocks nearby.

Time seemed to return to normal as the elevator behind us exploded in a ball of sound and fire that would have deafened a human. Thankfully, vampires seemed to have tougher eardrums, even if we could hear things far more easily.

My confusion over what had happened didn't last long, as I heard the Hunters shouting to one another.

"They're still alive!"

"Shoot them!"

"Get to the bomb! Detonate it before they stop it!"

"Are you crazy? I'm not here to martyr myself! I'm a cop, not a suicide bomber!"

Getting off the ground from where Melissa had tossed me, I lifted up my shotgun and proceeded to shoot the man who said that first. He was thrown back from the force of the magically enhanced shotgun blast, and I immediately moved behind one of the concrete pillars of the garage to avoid the resulting spray of gunfire.

"Fuck the police," I muttered, ready to kill each and every last one of these terrorist sons of bitches.

There were a lot of hunters down here, and even the ones disguised as delivery boys pulled out Uzis and submachine guns to start firing at us. It was a blessing this place didn't have any bystanders present. In the forest of cars, stone columns, and concrete lit by fluorescent lights, this parking garage was still a battlefield that favored our enemies.

Even so, I saw them lose one member after another thanks to Thoth shooting them with his rifle. He was hitting them with inhuman accuracy, only slowed down by the fact that he was using much of his super-speed to reload his rifle and dodge between pillars. I wasn't nearly as fast, but I had experience as a soldier and wasn't using antique weaponry either.

"This is how we do it in the army, assholes!" Grabbing a grenade from my bandolier, I hurled it like a pro among the hunters shooting up the place, and the resulting explosion took out six of them at one time. They were so huddled together that half of them were thrown to the ground or disorientated in one go. Tossing my shotgun on the ground, I left the comfort of cover and started walking toward the group with two pistols drawn, firing one shot after another into the crowd of hunters.

Strangely, time once more seemed to slow down around me and I got to step out of the way of one of the standing hunters firing his assault rifle at me as well as step past a grenade hurled in my direction before knocking it back in their direction. I could get used to this John Woo thing I had going here.

I had about three seconds to enjoy my success in tearing the hunters a new one before time suddenly returned to normal and I found myself full of hot lead. Forget what the movies show you about vampires just shrugging off bullets. They frigging hurt! I had about a dozen bullet holes in my body. I fell to my knees, howling in agony while still continuing to fire.

That had not gone like I'd thought it would.

"The blasphemer is down!" one of the hunters shouted. "Let us fini—"

He didn't get to say anything else before Thoth shot him too. The rest concentrated their fire on Thoth's position behind a yellow Mercedes, pinning my creator as they filled it with hundreds of bullets. One of them also tossed a grenade at it, sending him on the run. Unfortunately, they still had numbers enough to send someone after me in my moment of vulnerability. I tried to move, but I had bullets in my shoulders and legs, and two near my heart. If they'd been any closer, I would have been effectively staked.

Not good.

That was when a black hunter who looked like my cousin Dre come forward with a flamethrower on his back. He then spoke in a deep, James Earl Jones-like voice. "You're going to pay for all of the men you killed, Parasite. The holy flames of God are going to end your accursed existence."

"Keep it in church, chief." It wasn't the most badass line to go out on, but it was all I could think of.

Fire was a bad way to go.

Especially for an immortal.

"I'm sorry, Sean." Melissa came up from behind me and sliced the bastard's head clean off with a single stroke of the katana. She then moved at lightning speed to the last of the hunters, cutting them down one after the other. One of them seemed to recognize her and pulled a pin on a grenade, looking like he was trying to take them both out. She just ran away, leaving him to explode with yet another delivery van.

All in all, there were probably about thirty dead bodies around us in the end. It was a massacre, and worse than anything Detroit had seen since the gang wars during the Great Economic Collapse. Even so, I was glad we'd done it, since despite all the grenades flying around, nothing building-destroying had gone off.

But I couldn't enjoy it right now. The scent of blood was in the air, a massive amount of it, and it was overwhelming all reason. Crawling on my hands and knees due to the painful burning rounds in my flesh, I went from body to body, tearing at them to drink the still-dead blood inside. I slurped blood from their wounds until my body managed to force out all of the bullets and heal itself. It was ugly and sick, but I felt stronger and better fed than I had in years. Corpse juice was, after all, still human blood.

"That's disgusting," Melissa said, looking at me.

I looked back at her, spitting out the arm I'd chewed on. "Tell me you're not just barely holding back from going into these guys."

Melissa looked away, clearly queasy. "I knew some of these people. Their names. Their families. Ezekiel, the one with the flamethrower, was a man I went to school with."

"And they were ready to blow up a building full of gullible tourists," I said, standing up and looking down at my bullet-hole-filled shirt. "You're buying me another one of these, Thoth. I just saved your casino, that's the least you can do for me."

Thoth came out from behind one of the cars, limping, with his right leg all but destroyed by gunfire, and bullets in his left shoulder blade. "I'll give you a lot more than a shirt for your role in thwarting this. It's the least I can do."

"That's for damned sure," I said, hoping I could move out of the damn trailer park I was currently living in. I mean, a vampire in a trailer park sounds like an A&E show waiting to happen, and I didn't want to be the subject of it.

"First we need to make sure the bomb is disarmed and to see what we can learn from any survivors," Thoth said, still clutching his enchanted rifle.

"*What* survivors?" I asked, surveying the carnage around me.

That was when the sole remaining delivery van's back doors burst open and a young white man dressed like Kurt Cobain jumped out. He started running for the stairwell, not thinking clearly given he intended to get away from a trio of vampires (two with super-speed) on foot. He might have gotten away with it if he'd tried to drive away, though it was possible he didn't have the keys.

Thoth lifted up his rifle and fired.

The survivor stopped dead in his tracks.

"I have the detonator to the bomb!" the survivor shouted, obviously lying. "You don't want to kill me."

"You're quite wrong about that," Thoth said. "However, you might yet escape from this alive."

"He might?" I asked, looking at Thoth skeptically. I wasn't the mad-dog killer type, but screw these guys.

"Oh yes," Thoth said, his voice cold. "Would you do me the favor of interrogating him?"

I smiled, getting his meaning.

CHAPTER NINE

I held the surviving hunter up by his arms as the two of us floated two hundred feet in the air above the Apophis. Fireworks were going off in the background as part of the impromptu show by the (probably) fake Freddie Mercury, which was actually pretty good. I mean, Queen wasn't usually my cup of tea, but the guy was good.

"Oh God, oh God," the sole survivor said, repeating over and over again. It was painful to listen to.

"Tell me who helped you get into the casino, where Renaud is, and whatever else you're planning."

"Screw you, parasite!" the sole survivor said, defiant. "You killed all my ... ahh!"

He started screaming when I dropped him and let us both start dropping toward the ground. I grabbed him and started floating us both slowly back up around fifty feet from the ground. A couple of tourists on the ground took pictures, thinking it was part of the show.

"What was that?" I asked, pausing. "I'm sorry, I couldn't hear you over all the wind up here."

The sole survivor threw up and I grimaced, hoping that didn't hit anyone down below.

"I, I—"

I dropped one hand.

"I'll talk! I'll talk! Jesus!" The sole survivor shouted, ironically almost causing me to drop the poor bastard again.

"Let's start with your name and can the prayer. You can do that when you get down," I said. "Play your cards right and you might walk out from this."

"Really?" the sole survivor gasped. "You're not going to kill me?"

"Sure," I said, not sure at all if that was the case or not. "You might even avoid jail time if I like what I hear. I might also kill you like those other bastards, and I think you'll find a martyr's death isn't as glamorous as they've described it."

Back when I'd been Thoth's head of security, he'd taught me quite a few things that had enhanced the training I'd received back in Iraq. One of these was, as he put it, the "lost art of interrogation." Working over a guy—or hell, torturing him—sometimes worked but often went disastrously wrong. After all, it made people hate you and more inclined to lie. If you *really* did a number on them, then they might actually start remembering things differently from reality, as the mind was a lot more fragile than people realized.

Don't ask how I learned that.

Thoth argued that it was good to scare the shit out of people and then give them a reason to want to work with you. It wasn't anything more complicated than Good Cop, Bad Cop really, but vampires had to be both. No one believed we weren't monsters, so we had to be the manipulative, emotionally abusive bastards we were during interrogations.

And it worked.

"All right," the sole survivor whispered. "I'll tell you everything I know. Please, just don't kill me."

"Name, dude."

"Dude?" the sole survivor asked. "You're a vampire who says dude?"

I dropped him five feet.

The sole survivor shouted. "My name is Reggie! Reggie Porter, I live on 2555 Iroquois Avenue in—"

"We have your wallet," I said, cutting him off. "Tell me about what the hell you were trying to accomplish here."

"It was the Vampire Knight!" Reggie said, actually crying now. "I don't know why we allied with him but as soon he talked, everything he said started to make sense. He said we needed to blow up the Apophis as a distraction."

I blinked. "A *distraction?*"

"He said the real danger from the Vampire Nation wasn't the younger ones but the Old Ones. He said if we destroyed the Apophis, then the entire city would be crippled and confused. Renaud would then hunt down and kill all of the Old Ones in the city. Without them to cover up the other vampires' crimes and keep the money going, then humanity would turn on the undead and kill them all."

He probably wasn't wrong. When the Bailout had come with the terms of humanity accepting the legality of vampires, giving them their own legal system separate from regular humanity's, and a dozen other rules, some politicians had argued it would just be better to kill them all and confiscate their wealth. After all, we were dead, so did we really have a legal right to all those hidden trillions?

"Can you please set me down now?" Reggie whined.

"No," I said simply. "Where the hell is Renaud?"

"How should I know!" Reggie shouted, now angry as much as scared. "He just popped in and popped out, sleeping with our wives and girlfriends when he wasn't telling us what to do. Hell, he was outright dating our previous head."

"Melissa?"

"Yeah, that's her!" Reggie said, sighing. "Stupid bitch never understood this was a war and … argh! You're breaking my hands."

"Be nice to the ladies," I said, simply. "Maybe someday, one of them will be nice back. If this is all you got, you might as well be road pizza."

Honestly, if this was all he had, I was inclined to drop him anyway. Renaud was proving to be pretty damn skeevy for a genocidal religious nut, but wasn't that always the way? It also bothered me that he'd apparently used his powers to make all of these guys into terrorists, though I suspected it hadn't taken much persuasion since Reggie didn't seem very repentant. It did cast a shadow on just what sort of relationship he and Melissa had, though.

"Wait! Wait!" Reggie shouted, practically begging. "There's more."

"I'm listening."

"We emptied out all of the Human Rights League's coffers for this job to pay off some vampire. A guy in a cowboy hat, real asshole, named Tom."

"Theodore Eaton?" I said, once more tightening my grip.

Reggie winced. "Yeah, that's the guy."

Vampire blood was already cold, but if it wasn't, then mine would have turned cold in an instant. It was almost too good to be true, but the HRL paying off that piece of garbage was just the sort of leverage I needed to get a death sentence handed down on him. Not even Ashura would want to protect him after she found out he was involved in anti-vampire terrorism.

I was about ready to take Reggie down when he continued talking. "There's a backup plan, too."

"A backup plan? What?"

"I don't know!" Reggie snapped. "All I know is Renaud was talking to some other vampires. Young ones. Guys he said the Old Ones had been kicking around every bit as much as humanity, which is bullshit if you ask me."

"Did he give a name for this group?" I asked, my voice measured. "Some kind of network?"

"*The* Network?"

"Yeah!"

"Goddammit!" I snapped, grimacing.

The Network was one of the few "spooky" groups I respected. It was a kind of mutual support—well, network which had emerged in the aftermath of the Bailout. All of the various supernaturals getting in touch in their daily lives and on the Internet now that they no longer had to hide what they were. The Network had actually fought to have supernaturals treated like any other citizen of the United States in hopes of getting out from under the thumb of the mafia-like racial leaders. The Old Ones had responded brutally during the Network Riots, and the organization had been reduced to a shadow of its former self.

Just as planned.

Still, there were a substantial number of members here in New Detroit, and if the organization was a shadow of its former self, then it was still in existence. I had played a part in bringing them to that state, and it was a source of considerable guilt for me. I would have refused to believe them involved—I had friends among them, after all—but the simple fact was plenty of them had reasons beyond class warfare to hate the Old Ones. There would be massacres in the street once this information came out.

Dammit.

"Can I go now?" Reggie said.

I was tempted to just find a nice spot with no pedestrians and drop the son of a bitch, but as bad as I was, I was a man of my word. Usually. Besides, I had bigger fish to fry.

Slowly levitating to the ground, I found myself next to Thoth, Melissa, Fatimah, and David. The four of them were behind a set of metal-grate barriers, which they'd used to provide themselves some privacy.

Thoth had changed out his damaged "sexy pirate" attire and put on one of his signature suits, this time a bright red. Melissa was wearing a conservative trench coat, blouse, and knee-length dress to replace the cheap sweats I'd bought her on the way here.

Fatimah was the one who I had changed the most, as she was now wearing a tight black leather corset, the kind only vampire women could pull off (since they didn't have to breathe), as well as a pair of achingly tight pants. It made me uncomfortable because, well, I considered her akin to a sister and she was looking like an Afro-American version of Bloodrayne.

"Doesn't Islam have a prohibition against wearing stuff like that?" I said, setting my feet down on the ground before tossing Reggie before Thoth's feet.

Fatimah snorted. "It has also has a prohibition against drinking blood and bisexuality, but I manage to get by."

"You totally lied to me," David said, pointing at me. "She has a frigging harem."

"Who doesn't?" Thoth asked, shrugging. "I mean among vampires that matter."

I glared at them. "Great, now you've corrupted my servant."

"You should turn him soon," Fatimah said, smiling. "He's enjoyable company. Very useful in explaining why everyone had to leave the building without ruining their night."

I felt my face in horror.

David raised his hands up. "I also have this great deal for how we can cover up all the dead bigots. We take the bodies out to some church or safe house of the HRL along with their bomb, then blow it up. We then have the guy here explain they were working on a bomb and it looks like they blew themselves up preparing for an attack of some kind. The vampires don't look like mass murderers and the terrorists look like—well, idiots."

"I'll never betray my people like that!" Reggie said, seemingly acquiring a case of amnesia.

"Fatimah?" Thoth asked.

Fatimah reached down and picked him up by the back of his shirt, holding him in front of Thoth.

Thoth pulled out long curved ivory dagger, I think it was called a kukri, and slit his wrist before holding Reggie's mouth open so he would be unable to resist drinking the blood. Seconds later, the wound on Thoth's wrist sealed up and Reggie was staring forward as if in a trance.

Thoth stared at him. "Do you hear me?"

"Yes," Reggie said.

Thoth said, "You are now my servant. Not my Bloodsworn, but a Bloodslave. You will never receive rebirth, but be forever in the service to vampiredom. You will lie about what we want you to lie about and do what we tell you to do. You will serve as food to our guests when we acquire it and obey their commands as if they are your own. Your life will be one of toil and subservience from this point on. Do you understand?"

"Yes," Reggie said.

"Good," Thoth said. "Run along to the security room to join your compatriots we found there. You'll be all receiving your new instructions shortly."

"I understand," Reggie said.

"I understand, master," Thoth said.

Reggie twitched before responding. "I understand, master."

Fatimah let him go.

The HRL terrorist turned around and started walking away.

"You should have just killed him," I said, watching in disgust.

"I am not feeling that merciful," Thoth said. "When I killed my owner, his pain was over in a minute, while mine has lasted lifetimes."

There wasn't much I could say to that. "Wait a damned minute. If you could just mind zap him that way, why did you have me interrogate him?"

Thoth shrugged. "Mind control is even worse for interrogations than torture. I've accidentally convinced people they're chickens or from ancient Egypt with the wrong word choice. Besides, you have a knack for breaking people."

I rolled my eyes. "Oh, gee, thanks."

"You're welcome," Thoth said.

Melissa's expression was troubled. "Reggie had a wife and six-year-old daughter back home."

"He should have thought about that before he decided to ruin both their lives as well as his," Fatimah replied, walking over and then placing her hand on Melissa's face.

Melissa practically jolted at Fatimah's touch. "Uh—"

Fatimah smiled. "Look upon the thousands of people gathered around this place and know they continue to draw breath because of you. You think of us as the predators, but we are actually humanity's protectors. We have helped bring many wars and conflicts to a swift close as well as helped safeguard the environment. We have nurtured cities, the arts, learning, and culture where human leaders would have had their people fall into superstition or poverty. Vampires are the shepherds of humanity."

"Yeah, the better to shear them," I said, not at all convinced by Fatimah's spiel. "New Detroit is one gigantic all-you-can-eat buffet, except the food comes to you and pays you for the privilege of eating it."

Melissa actually laughed at that and pulled away.

Fatimah withdrew her hand. "You're such a spoilsport, Peter. Though I suppose we should give you your death name now."

"What?" I asked.

"You have come to your power," Fatimah said. "Most impressive."

I had no idea what she was talking about.

"That time slowdown effect," Melissa said, staring at me. "I've never seen anything like it."

"The Time Gift is a rare but not unprecedented ability," Thoth explained. "It's a more powerful version of the manipulation of our auras to produce super-speed. Practitioners have been known to see into the future and the past, draw images off from objects, and manipulate the flow of time as you saw it."

"Will I be able to go back in time if I run eighty-eight miles per hour?" I asked.

"Only if you have a Flux Capacitor," Thoth said.

Fatima, David, and Melissa stared at him.

"What?" Thoth said.

"Yeah, well, I have no idea how I did that." I tried to remember the circumstances that had brought it about. I'd been thinking about the worst day of my life, and then someone had tried to blow me up. Neither were things I really wanted to repeat in order to figure out how to go back into instant replay mode.

"Did you learn anything about Renaud?" Fatimah asked.

I contemplated what I was going to say and hoped Thoth wasn't listening to my thoughts. "Yeah, Eaton's involved in this shit. He helped set up the attack on the Apophis in exchange for a big payoff. Also … Renaud is planning an attack on the Network."

Thoth raised an eyebrow. "The Network, are you sure?"

I nodded. "Absolutely."

"You should go warn them then," Thoth said. "I'll inform the voivode of Eaton's treachery. Take Melissa with you. She's earned a measure of our trust and still might be useful in tracking down Renaud before he strikes again."

"Great," I said, wondering why the hell I'd just lied for the Network. What had I gotten myself into?

CHAPTER TEN

I bought a brand new black sweatshirt and hoodie to go with a new pair of sweatpants from the Apophis gift shop. Aside from the gigantic ankh symbol on my chest, which practically announced to the world I was a vampire, it was nicer clothes than I was used to wearing lately. Thoth gave me his wallet's cash, and that turned out to be two thousand dollars. Pocket change for him, but enough to seriously improve my situation.

God, I hated being poor.

I could have probably taken a number of the Apophis's rentals or one of my creator's cars to visit the Network, but that wasn't going to improve my chances of getting anything out of them. The Network was mostly made up of poor and struggling vampires like me, but there were rakshasas, half-demons, fairies, shapeshifters, and others among them too.

If I walked in there looking like one of the establishment I'd get my ass handed to me. The Network might not have much power left, but there was a reason the Bogatyr didn't just go smashing up their meetings. So we took my Jeep Liberty instead.

Sitting in the driver's seat, I was very conscious of the fact Melissa was beside me, probably pondering how she'd just gone from being a woman desperate to protect humans from vampires to a spree killer in three seconds flat.

I didn't have the heart to tell her that was part and parcel of the vampire package. A vampire might feel immense guilt over being a killer, even kill himself over it, but the fact was we were made by biology to kill. The wiring that prevented most humans from even contemplating murder wasn't there anymore.

It had its upside.

David was in the back as before, but he was also next to a couple of duffle bags and a set of towels, which were covering up all the weapons Thoth had lent me. I wasn't exactly comfortable driving around even as vamp-friendly a town as New Detroit with the small arsenal in my backseat, but it was better than going into this situation unarmed.

Thoth had also made sure I had some extra protection, which I was grateful for. I relived that moment in perfect clarity too, despite it just being an hour ago and not really something I needed to re-experience.

"Take this," Thoth had said as I loaded the car. He handed me an ivory kukri covered in blood runes. It was beautiful, with an artistry I'd never felt before in a weapon.

"I'm not really a knife man," I said, sensing the power radiating from it. "You make that from an elephant?"

"I made it from my creator's arm."

I grimaced. "What the hell are you giving it to me for then?"

"Doubye had his arm torn off in a battle with lycanthropes in Haiti after they tried to free the island from his corruption of the Voudon faith," Thoth said. "I was still his slave and could do nothing about it, but as he recovered, I took his severed arm and boiled the flesh from it. I spent weeks carving it and pouring all of my hatred into it while praying to the Loa to give me the strength to do what needed to be done."

"Which was?"

"Stabbing it into his heart and killing him," Thoth said. "The ultimate sin among our kind."

"I thought only an Old One could kill an—" It dawned on me what he was saying. "Wait, it's that easy?"

Thoth frowned. "I wouldn't say killing an Old One with weapons made from another Old One's bones is easy, but yes, that's one way of getting around it."

I took the knife in hand and stared at it. "So, I could just kill you right now?"

Thoth didn't react. "Do you want to kill me, Peter?"

I sighed. "I'd say sometimes I do, but no, not even then. You pissed me off, though, when you didn't have my back. You should have stood by me."

Thoth closed my eyes. "Yes. I suppose I should have."

"You suppose right." I held the weapon tight. "So all I have to do is jam this into Renaud's chest and he's toast?"

Thoth paused. "Probably not. As you can imagine, this object has some great personal importance to me and I've been steadily enchanting it and adding to its power over the centuries. Renaud is an immensely powerful immortal, though."

"You're scared of him."

Thoth didn't deny it. "I don't expect you try and kill Renaud. In fact, if you see him, I advise you to run so we can call in a full-scale assault. I don't want you without protection, though. Time Gift or not."

"Yeah, well, I don't know how to use that."

"Not all vampires have daily vivid recollections of their past, Peter. You've had it for a long time now."

"Lucky me. And it's Stone now," I corrected him. "If I have to have one name, I'd like to at least be the coolest-sounding of my three."

"You are the rock on which New Detroit is built."

I shook my head. "Don't compare yourself to the messiah, T, that's just wrong."

I wasn't intending to use the dagger on Renaud. Vampires got stronger the more they aged, and seven hundred years old was a pretty big difference to try and cross even with automatic weapons. Hell, look how much good they'd done the HRL hunters. The knife was the perfect weapon for killing a much stronger but still young vampire, though.

Someone like Eaton.

Best of all, it would also look like some long-dead Old One did him in if they did any magic on his ashes. As far as I was concerned, it was Christmas. Weird how that holiday didn't give me the heebie-jeebies the way other uses of the Big J's name did. Maybe the fundamentalists were right about it getting too commercialized.

Nah.

"So, why did you lie to your creator?" Melissa asked, almost causing me to wreck.

"Huh, what?"

David looked up from reading his Kindle, still acting like all of this was perfectly normal. I had been the same way. Being one of the Bloodsworn was pretty normalizing to all sorts of crazy shit. I blamed the blood. "What did you lie about?"

"I didn't lie about anything!" I said. "How did you know?"

David paused. "Okay, Pet—er, Stone—that's a really bad way of trying to claim you didn't do something."

Melissa shrugged. "I picked it up from your thoughts over our connection."

"Dammit," I muttered. "That's not how the bond is supposed to work. It's supposed to one-way, you to me."

"Actually, she shouldn't be picking up anything from you at all," David pointed out. "Renaud made her rather than you."

"Yeah, well, I gave her my blood during her change, so I suppose Melissa has two daddies now," I said, trying to shrug it off. "Look it up on the Internet to see if it's ever happened before."

"Righto," David said, playing with his Kindle some more.

"You realize I'm not going to be so easily distracted," Melissa said. "Who are these Network people to you?"

"That's none of your business," I said, shaking my head. "Just because you weren't willing to blow up a bunch of Midwesterners spending their vacation money at the slots and pointing out the freaks doesn't mean I don't know that you're a vampire hunter."

"Oh, is *that* why you punched me in the throat!" David said from the back. "I was wondering what the hell that was all about."

Melissa paused. "I lied to you."

"No kidding," I said.

"My family *was* killed by vampires," Melissa said, changing her tone. "It took me a while to find out, and I had to use a witch, but the drunk driver who slammed into their car had been hypnotized into doing it."

I held back my retort—that her father had it coming for being an anti-vampire bigot. Right or wrong, the fact was that you wanted to avenge your family. "You ever find out which vampire did it?"

"No," Melissa said, staring out onto the road.

We were entering the bad part of town now, which we'd have to cross in order to get to the place where we were going: the *really* bad part of town.

Old Detroit.

"I looked for a long time and dealt with a lot of people I shouldn't have in order to find out who he might have been. I even let myself be bled by vampires." Melissa said it like it she had performed some great sacrifice versus something guys and girls paid two hundred bucks a bite for at the Velvet Room.

"And a dead end?"

"Yeah," Melissa said. "I devoted myself to trying to oppose vampire special privileges and go after those who slipped through the cracks of the legal system. Also to developing a cure for those who wanted to transform back."

"Yeah, pray back the day," David said. "Vampirism isn't a disease, Melissa.'"

Melissa didn't respond to that. "I was already starting to regret those feelings towards the end. I killed someone who didn't deserve it."

"You don't *accidentally* kill someone when you track down and murder them," I said, disgusted with her evasions. "Thoth told me about the alleged rapist who turned out to just be some girl's boyfriend."

Melissa actually looked stricken. "Her parents contacted me and told me the whole story. I interviewed a half-dozen people from cops to the local judge to the girl herself. All of them repeated the same basic story. That he was a monstrous predator who needed to be put down. That he'd caused the immense amount of bruising and abuse she'd endured. That he'd even caused her to lose the baby she had by her good Christian boyfriend."

I grimaced. This story was starting to sound familiar. "Let me guess. The girl's baby was actually the vampire's, and the bruises were from her parents trying to make her lose it. That or to make sure she was going to give you the story they wanted."

"They succeeded," Melissa said. "Apparently, it's not abortion if it's a half-human monstrosity."

David looked especially pissed off by her story. "So you tracked him down and killed him."

Melissa sighed. "It was ridiculously easy. He was at his mother's house in a closet. I pulled him out while he was unconscious, put him on a tarp, hammered a wooden stake in his heart, and cut off his head. His mother said it was better this way."

"His mother? How old was he? Really?" I asked.

It wasn't often I said a Black woman looked white as a ghost, but this was one of those occasions. "Seventeen. He'd only been a vampire for a few months. An older vampire had changed him while passing through and trained him just enough to hunt on his own. He mostly lived on animal blood and his girlfriend."

"How did you feel when you found out the truth?"

Melissa stared at the road. "I wanted to die. I wanted to bring up the parents on charges of murder and I wanted to confess my crime to the police. I wanted to atone for what I'd done even if I never could."

"Why didn't you?" David asked, his voice acidic. He'd really come around to the view of "we all have to be free if anyone is to be free." I felt kind of guilty because I didn't think half as well of vampires as he did.

"My fellow HRL members convinced me not to," Melissa said, sickened. "They told me it wouldn't do any good. That it had been an honest mistake. That I would just ruin all the good work the HRL was doing in showing the crimes of the actually-guilty vampires and would become a tool to make them even more legally unaccountable."

"So you chickened out," I said.

"Yeah," Melissa said. "I didn't want to go to jail for the rest of my life and was willing to accept an excuse, any excuse, not to do it."

"Is this when you started screwing Renaud?" I asked again. I didn't know why it bothered me so much. Well, actually, I knew, but I didn't want to admit it. That wasn't happening.

Melissa stared at me. "Fuck you. That's none of your business."

"Just saying, we're going to kill the guy. Don't quite see the appeal there myself."

"Renaud came to me when I was on the verge of resigning from the HRL. He approached me first and said that we needed to take a more proactive approach against the undead. That we could build a better society where the guilty vampires were punished and the good allowed to go on with their unlives by destroying the Vampire Nation. To do that, we had to target the leaders rather than the general citizenry."

That was actually useful information and indicated Renaud

might not just be the random genocide-seeking psychopath Thoth described him as. Unfortunately, even if he wasn't, he was still willing to kill thousands to achieve his aims. "Go on."

"He gave me his blood and I became his lover as well as partner in the hunt. There were other women he was with, but somehow, that didn't seem important at the time." Melissa paused. "We destroyed a lot of vampires together. The voivodes of New York, Jersey City, Pittsburgh, and a lot of their courts' membership."

I didn't know how to react. "I would have heard of that."

"I understand they're supposed to have been summoned back by the Council of Ancients," Melissa said. "It's a cover for the fact that they're all dead."

"You realize there's no way the Vampire Nation will let you live if that comes out," I said, processing what she'd said.

"I'm prepared for what comes next," Melissa said, her voice even. "Even though we managed to do all that, though, Renaud felt it wasn't enough. He'd been regenerating after a bomb hit him during World War II and it seemed vampire numbers had gotten so out of control, there was no way for any one man to deal with them all."

"That's when he came up with another plan to get humanity to turn on us," I said, finishing for her.

"Yeah," Melissa said. "I thought he was brooding, cursed, and tragic, but it turned out he was just a controlling evil asshole sleeping with half the women in the group."

David actually laughed at her. "You got Twilighted."

Melissa leaned back beyond her chair and gave David the finger.

It actually wasn't that uncommon. A century of vampire-controlled media had done a lot to de-fang us, so to speak, and the reality was less than what a lot of people hoped it to be. God knew I was still waiting for my nightclub and spooky mansion where I sipped blood from wine glasses.

But that wasn't important now. "I'm not going to turn you in and neither is David."

"I'm not?" David asked.

"You're not," I commanded him. Really, I was surprised I'd resisted doing this to him before. It was a lot easier on the mind than I'd expected. "I've got enough problems right now without adding 'protecting Old One murderer' to my list. Just keep it to yourself and we'll call it our little secret."

Melissa seemed stunned. "Thank you."

"You're welcome."

We were now well into Old Detroit, the place where all the people who hadn't been willing to get with the new vampire-ruled paradigm had been sent. The name was a bit of a misnomer, since much of the original city had been redeveloped and this was actually a part that reached just outside of town. It was, however, pretty familiar to me since it was exactly the sort of overcrowded crime-ridden hellhole I'd grown up in.

Detroit had something of an unfair reputation as, economic difficulties aside, it had been a place with strong community ties and people who were willing to fight for their city. Neither of its successor states had any of that going for them. The people trapped in Old Detroit were there either because they hated vampires or because they were vampires who'd pissed off the Old Ones. New Detroit was a glittering piece of red zirconium promising a better life while being built on fraud and lies.

The building I was looking for was a former church that had been deconsecrated and turned into a bar. It was surrounded by old beat-up Harley Davidson motorcycles and had a couple of snipers visibly patrolling on the rooftop, if you weren't yet understanding what sort of place Old Detroit was. The name of the place, The Razor, was prominently displayed across the front in half-functioning neon.

"This isn't going to go well," I muttered, parking my car across the street. "I never did answer you why I was so protective of the Network, did I?"

"No," Melissa said.

"Yeah, well, my ex-girlfriend is the head of it."

CHAPTER ELEVEN

"Your ex-girlfriend? Really?" Melissa asked as all three of us got out of the car.

"Elisha Hernandez isn't the head of the entire Network, obviously," I said, trying to downplay what she was. "She's just the head of the local branch."

"The branch in the biggest supernatural hub in the world," David said, smirking. "You could basically call her the Princess Leia of the Resistance to the Council of Ancients' Evil Empire."

I gave my servant a stare that could have melted steel. "Really, David?"

"Hey, they'd take the evil empire thing as a compliment," David said, defensively.

They probably would. "Yeah, well, it's complicated, but if anyone can find out where Renaud is hanging out in the city, then it's very likely her people."

I still remembered the taste of Elisha's blood in my mouth and the pleasure of her fangs in my neck. I remembered pressing her down against the bed, up against walls, and things that wouldn't fly on Skinemax. Vampires didn't really think of sex the way human beings did anymore. The Bite, essentially, reduced sex to foreplay. It was good and fun, don't get me wrong, but really just the lead-up for the good stuff.

Even so, we'd had a lot of sex over the years.

"Why'd you break up?" Melissa asked. "Which I know is none of my business—"

"You're absolutely correct."

"But given we're entering into a vampire-run bar, I'd rather know if she's going to start shooting you on sight."

There was actually a decent chance of that. "This isn't so much a vampire bar as a neutral ground for the poor and dispossessed of Detroit."

"Way to duck the question," Melissa said, not stepping across the street until I answered her question.

I closed my eyes. "In the end I had to make a choice. That choice didn't go down well with a lot of the people here."

"What kind of choice?" Melissa asked.

"A stupid one." I had to choose between fighting in their war or staying on the sidelines. I'd stayed on the sidelines, which was probably a good thing since I'd been spying on them nearly my entire time with them. I still regretted the way things had ended with Elisha, despite the fact it was entirely her fault we broke up.

Wow, I was a douchebag.

"What kind of reception can we expect in there?" Melissa asked.

I shook my head. "It depends. I was pretty friendly with some of the Network's people even after I broke up with Elisha. Not all of them agreed with her politics or the direction she was taking the organization. Others hate me and think I'm part of the establishment."

"Because your creator *is* the establishment?" David said.

"More like heavily invested in it," I said. "But yeah, that and I kind of told them they could take their organization and take a running leap out the front door at noon."

Melissa snorted. "Is that all?"

"Yeah," I said, walking to the front door. The snipers didn't shoot at us, but one of them did aim at me, which told me all I needed to know about how I was going to be received here.

There was a time when I'd been pretty damn sympathetic to the Network. Still was, since I was possibly covering up their involvement with Renaud. I'd learned a lot since then, including why the entire organization was one big joke on its members, but that didn't keep me from sympathizing with the little guy. It was one-third Black Panthers, one-third Occupy Wall Street, and one-third street gang.

My kind of people.

"Stay down and don't draw attention to yourself," I said, taking note of the two dozen motorcycles out front. There were just as many cars up and down the block, including our own. The Razor was a temporary shelter for those of Old Detroit's supernaturals without a place to go. "This isn't your scene."

"You'd be surprised what my scene was," Melissa said, taking my arm. "Vampire hunters usually don't get their prey by hanging around church."

"Don't mention that either." I pointed a finger at her for emphasis.

"What about me?" David asked. "Any tips for fitting in?"

"Don't piss anyone off," I said.

"And if I do?"

"I don't know you from Renfield."

David frowned at that.

As we reached The Razor's wooden front doors, I heard an old-fashioned jukebox playing "Bela Lugosi's Dead" by Bauhaus from inside. The Network sure did love the classics. Opening the doors, I entered into a church that had been turned into a combination of a bar, strip club, and impromptu town hall.

The Razor's main hall had been cleaned out of pews, and in their place was a dozen picnic tables stolen from New Detroit Central Park. There was also a set of pool tables being played on, with at least one of the players floating over the board for a better shot. Replacing the altar was a large bar with rows of various spirits in a cathedral of booze, blood, and mixtures of both.

The lights were jury-rigged, with a set of Christmas lights adding to the ambience. There was a slight red tinge to the illumination, which made everything a good deal more ominous. Just as I remembered, the jukebox was to one side, and now switching over to Nightwish's "Century Child." The strip club portion of the place came about because someone had stabbed steel poles into a couple of the tables, and a few of the bar's customers were taking advantage of them. They shed their clothes to dance just for the hell of it, like we were in *Return of the Living Dead*.

As for the inhabitants? They were a bunch of freaks. There were no two ways around that. As Thoth said, supernaturals had developed their own culture independent of so-called regular society, and that meant they tended to be a little on the rougher or scarier side. Just about everyone was sporting black leather, chains, spikes, and all manner of piercings. There was also less need to employ glamours to disguise inhuman features. I saw people who had red skin, horns, and tails, as well as those whose creation hadn't kept them from looking like walking corpses.

"Strange," Melissa said, surveying the place even as she looked like Janet entering Doctor Frank-N-Furter's castle for the first time.

"A bit of an understatement, don't you think?" I said, walking down the main pathway between the tables to the bar.

"No, I mean it's the first time I've ever been in a place like this and it didn't smell like a men's room. There's no scent of smoke either."

"Yeah, The Razor has a strict no smoking policy."

"How do they enforce that?" Melissa asked.

"The werewolves eat anybody who does it," I said, noticing there wasn't much of the old gang here. I caught a couple of glimpses of people I vaguely recognized, but there was no sign of the group I used to hang out with post-creation. I wondered if they were all dead.

"All right," I said, taking an entirely pointless deep breath. "Everyone play it cool. I know the lady who tends the bar, but we can't show any kind of weakness here. This is the kind of place where people will say they're going to kick your teeth in and then do it."

"I think you're overestimating just how dangerous this place is," Melissa said.

"What?" I asked, doing a double-take.

"Most of these places are safe havens for a reason. They're built on fundamentally different sorts of rules than dens for criminals. Most of the people here probably just want to have a good time in the company of their fellow supernaturals."

I rolled my eyes, wondering where someone less than a night old got off telling me about how not dangerous this place was.

"Pete! My baby boy!" A shrill but pleasant voice, like a Hindi Fran Drescher, shouted from nearby.

"Ah hell," I muttered. This was going to suck.

I found myself wrapped up in six arms from behind, which lifted me up like a rag doll, then spun around and hugged by an Indian woman six inches taller than me as well as a helluva lot stronger. Mama Kali was beautiful. She looked to be in her early thirties and she kept her hair up in a hairstyle approaching a beehive in size.

Kali was wearing an outrageous long ruffled red dress that looked like something more appropriate for prom night. The extra arms coming out of her sides appeared and disappeared at her will, leaving only fashionable holes whenever she wasn't using them.

Rakshasas were funny that way.

"Oh, hey!" I said, unable to resist being treated like her long-lost nephew. "How ya doing, Kali? Glad to see you're still around."

I was, sort of.

"You are so cute!" Kali said, dropping me. She then pinched my cheek and ruined any credibility I might have had as a hardass. "You've also come into your power, I can sense it! I remember when you first walked into my bar, I said, that is a vampire who is going places! Which you still have time to do! Someday!"

I rubbed the back of my head. "Uh, thanks."

"Show no weaknesses, huh?" Melissa said, practically giggling.

"Heya!" David said. "Long time no see."

"You know her?" I said, looking at David.

"Oh yeah, she DJ-ed my prom," David said. "You know, back when she was just the strangest lady on my block."

"David!" Mama Kali said, stretching out her arms. "Why hasn't this poor lug made you a vampire yet?"

"He's only been my servant for three months!" I snapped. "Why is everyone thinking that's long enough?"

Mama pointed at me with three hands. "When you meet the right one, you know."

I covered my face. "Please don't say that."

"So, I take it you're the owner?" Melissa asked, her voice friendly and cheerful.

Kali stopped to look at Melissa, raising an eyebrow as if surveying her soul. "Interesting. And you are?"

"Melissa. Just Melissa."

"Yes, Just Melissa, I am Mama Kali, mistress and proprietor of The Razor. Whenever there are wayward supernaturals, lost souls, and those cast out from their homes, I am here to lend them a helping hand or six. It is my pleasure to welcome any friend or family of Pete's to my demesne."

"She's not my friend," I said, immediately regretting saying it.

"But she does share your blood," Kali said, her black eyes seeming to penetrate the soul. "As well as the blood of the Crusader."

Melissa's eyes widened. "You know?"

"Shh!" I said, looking over my shoulder. "We're trying to keep that on the down low."

Kali snorted. "Good luck with that. Jumping Jack Flash has been prophesizing all night about the Crusader and the terrible doom he's going to bring to the city."

Kali gestured with her head to one of the nearby tables, where a beak-nosed white man in a white shirt, large coat, and oversized fedora was drinking a thick tankard of what looked like green beer. Jumping Jack Flash was someone I recognized and something of an enigma. No one could really tell what sort of supernatural he was, and he was usually too addled to give any concrete answer.

Jumping Jack Flash leaned over to kiss a bald man with a dog collar around his neck before speaking. "The doom of the Apophis shall come down in flames and fire, smiting the civilization of New Detroit. The ibis, the soldier, and the inquisitor shall thwart this or not. Maybe there will be a heartbreak as good men aid evil with betrayals! Oh, and there will be turmoil in the Middle East."

I stared at him. "He's a bit late on a few of those. I suspect the last one to be accurate, though."

"Jumping Jack Flash doesn't prophesize what will *be* like a true seer, just what *might* be. Which, in most cases, just means he's a good guesser."

"There are people who can prophesize what will be?" Melissa asked. "No possibility of changing it?"

"Oh yes," Kali said, nodding. "We supernaturals kill them as soon as they're identified."

Melissa opened her mouth to raise an objection, then closed it.

"The virgin will buy me a beer," Jumping Jack Flash said to David.

"I'm not a virgin," David said. "And I'm not buying you a beer."

"The liar will buy me a beer or I shall speak it to all the hills," Jumping Jack Flash said, raising an eyebrow. "Also, about how you once took your mother's—"

"Get that guy a beer, would you?" David said, reaching for his wallet and checking its contents. "Uh, Stone will pay you."

I gave him a sideways look. "Why did I make you my servant again, David?"

"Because the only thing worse than working at a Qwik & Shop as a vampire is working at one without someone technically lower?" David suggested.

"Technically?" I asked.

"Oh, you work at a Qwik & Shop?" Kali asked, putting two hands in front of her mouth. "Why didn't you come to me! I could have saved you from that fate worse than damnation!"

I didn't argue with her there. "I wasn't exactly sure I'd still be welcome here. Not after the incident. I didn't know how many of my old associates here were still holding a grudge."

"There aren't many of those left," Kali said, sighing. "So sad."

"I see," I said, taking a deep breath.

"Almost all of them have moved uptown and taken jobs with the establishment," Kali said. "Midtown sells our culture and heritage for American dollars. Most of us have just stopped trying to fight it."

"The Network allows that?" I asked, disgusted.

"You know what the Network really is," Kali said, showing she'd figured out the truth I'd figured out long ago. Not difficult for a woman who could read another's sins. "It's those who feel it shouldn't be about making money that bother me. They refuse to accept the cause is lost or, if you think about it, won in an unsatisfying way."

I picked up on Kali's hint. "I need to speak with Elisha about some things. How badly has she gone off the deep end?"

"The ocean of the soul is a funny thing," Kali said. "You can always go deeper."

"Until you drown," I said.

"Drinks, Soldier of Time!" Jumping Jack Flash shouted. "Drinks and I shall share the secret of Atlantis's destruction! I shall share what I learned from the bodhisattva Jim Morrison and how to contact the ghost of Jimi Hendrix! I will tell you how to make a fool and his money part ways."

I pulled out my wallet and gave Kali a hundred-dollar bill. "I'll give you this if you can get him to shut up."

"And that is one of them," Jumping Jack Flash said.

Kali smiled at the bill and stretched it between a pair of her hands. "Qwik & Shop pays a lot better than I expected."

"I came into an inheritance," I said, wishing I hadn't brought it out. "Is Elisha still plugged into the underground?"

"My dear, she *is* the underground," Kali said, shaking her head. "Be wary of seeing things as they were versus how they are."

"What the hell is that supposed to mean?" I asked, sick and tired of these word games.

"Peter?" Elisha's voice was a blast from the past.

I turned around. Elisha was standing there in an uncharacteristic pantsuit with her raven hair pulled back in a severe bun. Elisha was Latina in origin, her mother Puerto Rican and her father half-Mexican, half-Italian. Her skin was a fairly light shade of brown, but still to my taste. It was strange seeing her dressed like that since my last memories of her were very different.

Then I had another flashback.

Goddammit.

CHAPTER TWELVE

I found my mind once more moving to the past and I wondered how to stop doing that. I needed to stay focused on the present. These kinds of distractions were going to get me killed, especially when the person in front of me very much wanted to kill me.

At least the last we met.

In my vision, it was almost two years ago. The Razor was decked out like a fortress with all of the tables covered in armaments. All of the still-strong Network's soldiers were prepping for war on Elisha's command. Elisha had a wilder style back then, like a sexy Marxist guerilla. She was dressed in a green camo tank top with blue jeans and a leather jacket. Her long straight dark hair hung down to her shoulders and her dad's Special Forces beret rested slightly to one side of her head.

Elisha was holding a shotgun as the rest of her gang was prepping their weapons behind her. There were vampires, spriggans, succubi, dhampyr, two werecats, a wereraven, and a witch. The Network had already lost so many people, it was horrifying to think they were going to lose more in a pointless battle.

Two days ago, the Santa Muerta gang, a jumped-up crew of hedge mages and Bloodsworn with delusions of grandeur, had killed two members of the Network as a lesson to stay out of their business. The Santa Muerta had decided they were going to run Old Detroit's criminal enterprises, and for that to happen, they need to get rid of Elisha and her crew.

The Network wasn't a group of criminals by inclination, but to provide any kind of support to the supernatural world's less fortunate meant they raised money through illicit means. That meant drug-dealing, prostitution, a lower class sort of gambling than the casinos offered, and sometimes worse.

Tonight was worse.

"This is a bad idea, Elisha," I said, trying to figure out a way to convince her to abandon this fight before she got her people killed. I didn't have any doubt they could take down the Santa Muerta, but they would suffer casualties, and that would leave them vulnerable to the next group wanting to carve a place in Old Detroit's rapidly expanding underworld.

I looked at Jumping Jack Flash, who was playing with a deck of cards, seemingly unconcerned that this group was going to war, then at Kali. Kali's expression was unhappy even as she served everyone a round of free drinks.

Of the group, I thought she was the only one besides me who suspected that this conflict was prearranged to continue driving down property values so the Old Ones could expand their construction project. The problem was, I'd tried to explain this to them and found myself talking to deaf ears.

In retrospect, I should have thought more about the differences between who I was and who they were. I was wearing a fine suit, not as expensive as the kind Thoth wore, but still a shit ton nicer than the kind of clothes I was reduced to wearing now. I was an outsider to them, one that wasn't ever going to win them over with words.

But I'd tried.

"It's a horrible idea, but it still has to be done, Iraq," Elisha said, using her pet name for me. "Blood has been spilled and honor needs to be satisfied."

"You're being used." I tried to explain the situation to her. "The Old Ones don't want you or the Muerta here in Detroit, so they're playing you against one another."

It was how the Old Ones did things. When you reached a certain age, you learned how not to fight your own battles but to get your enemies to fight each other. It had only been two years since the Uprising, when the Council's agents had manipulated the Network into attacking their representatives, justifying a major crackdown.

"Don't you think I know that?" Elisha said, coming up to my face. "Don't you think I know exactly who benefits from all this?"

"Then why—"

"Because we don't have a choice!" Elisha snapped. "We have to war for turf and defend it because there are people out there who need us. Younger vampires who don't know what the rules are, what is going to happen to them if they disobey them, and who have no place to go if they don't have the Network. Families are still getting driven out of their homes all across the country because they're found out as supernatural. The government wants us all segregated in the Rust Belt cities because it's convenient for them and the Old Ones. It's supernatural apartheid."

I did my best to not roll my eyes at the comparison. Elisha loved her hyperbole, and the differences were probably not going to register to her when she was trying to avenge her dead friends. I knew that kind of revenge—I had taken it, and it felt damned good—but it wasn't going to help matters. I knew the horrible terrible secret of the Network and why everything they were doing was pointless.

"There's another option," I whispered.

"What?"

This was an even worse idea than theirs, but it was the one I could think of that didn't leave a bunch of fresh corpses. "You should try to make peace with the Muerta."

"Ha!" Elisha scoffed. "You're insane. You've spent too much time in the Apophis, sucking blood from the tits of hookers."

There was a general agreement from the other supernaturals in the room and I could tell I was losing them.

"You can join your strength together and force the Old Ones to take you seriously. As you're divided, you won't be able to do anything against them, which is how they like it. If you kill them, you'll also just be inviting in more people to pick up the slack and then you'll have to kill their replacements and so on until you're bled white."

"You know the story of how I became a vampire, but not everyone here does," Elisha said, not talking so much to me as at me.

"Please, baby, don't make this a speech."

"I was born the daughter of a single-parent family here in Detroit—"

"Oh God, you're making this a speech." I covered my face, knowing this wasn't going to go anywhere good.

"I struggled with anger, depression, and feelings of violence growing up. Vampires weren't public back then, only myths and creatures of fiction, so I never suspected the blood of the undead ran through my still-living veins. I was a dhampyr, a half-vampire created by my mother being forced into servitude by my monstrous father. When she became pregnant, he abandoned her to poverty and a child whose flaws she had no idea how to deal with."

None of this had anything to do with our situation, but there was no sense in interrupting her now. The rest of the audience, her speech's real target, was eating out of the palm of her hand.

Elisha stared at me. "When the Bailout happened and the vampires revealed themselves, my mother broke down. The shock of the monsters haunting her nightmares being real was too much for her. She revealed the truth of my accursed birth on her deathbed. I tracked my wayward father down, finding a string of broken lives and shattered minds along the way. When I found him, he attacked me, changed me, and left me for the sun. Now, he sits as one of the city's secret masters and a courtier to the voivode."

"Elisha—"

"My story is not an uncommon one, and every supernatural here has a similar one. We've had to fight for what little we have here and against those who would take it away." Elisha handed me my shotgun. "You talk like one of them, you know. You didn't used to. Back when you were a servant, I thought you were special. I wish I had created you myself rather than that walking snake, Thoth. You have a choice. You can fight with us for a better future or go back to your friends in uptown."

Elisha didn't know about my brother. In all of our time together, I'd never told her. So, she didn't expect my eyes to darken as I shoved the gun back to her. "I'm done fighting for other people's turf."

Six months later I was exiled and the Network was barely holding together after driving the Muerta from the city. They'd ended up making peace and sharing the city's drug profits.

I hated being right.

Looking at her now, I could see that the past two years had changed her. The revolutionary fire was still in her eyes, but it had been dulled into a low burning flame over an ashen pit. It said something about how vampirism changed you that I was starting to think with those sort of flourishes. But there was something about

Elisha that inspired the poetic side of my soul. I shared her anger about the excesses of supernatural society, and wished I could have helped her. I'd just lost too many loved ones fighting other people's wars.

"Is this where you slap me in the face and call me an asshole?" I asked, trying to break the ice.

"This isn't a movie, Iraq," Elisha said, sighing. "We're a little past the point of white hot anger followed by forgiveness. Right now, whenever I think about our past relationship, all I feel is numb."

Ouch.

I deserved that, probably, but it still hurt.

"I see," I said.

"Hey Elisha," David said, waving to her. "How's things?"

"Could be better, David," Elisa said, giving a forced but sincere smile. "Still working at the Qwik & Shop?"

"Yeah, it's the only place where no one gives enough of a shit to fire me," David said. "I even got Pete a job there."

"No!" Elisha said. "That's horrifying!"

"I know!" Kali added. "Peter, you poor thing!"

"Get this—he actually tries to do his job," David said, sniggering. "It's *hilarious*."

"All right." I stepped among them. "That's enough, everyone. I've had enough of 'make fun of the black vampire' day."

"You're not the only black vampire here," Melissa corrected, amused at my parade of embarrassments.

That was when Elisha walked up close to her, the Network leader's posture turning hostile and predatory. "Don't I know you?"

Melissa immediately tensed. "No, I'm sure you don't. I admit, I do have one of those faces, though."

Elisha narrowed her eyes. "No, you don't."

I stepped between them quickly. "Elisha, need to talk."

"I can't imagine what you think we could talk about after all this time," Elisha said, putting her hands on her hips.

"Yeah, he's got a lot of guts coming back here after what he pulled," David said, nodding along.

I looked back at him. "Listen, *Star Wars* references are applicable to almost everything, but not anything involving the supernatural."

"The Force is supernatural," David pointed out.

I stared at him and he actually hid behind Kali.

"Worst servant ever," I muttered. "This is important, Elisha, and not something that can be discussed in public."

Elisa stared at me and I could still see the hurt in her eyes from when I betrayed her. When I'd heard about how many Network agents had been killed in her fight with the Muerta, I'd beaten myself up for weeks, trying to think if I could have turned that untrained underpowered group of rabble into something that could have fought them. Whether I, alone, could have made a difference.

I know Elisha thought I could have. In fact, I'd be very surprised if Elisha didn't just tell me to get the hell out. Even if Kali owned and operated the bar, almost the entirety of the clientele was Network. The very fact that she was a dhampyr turned vampire and probably three times as strong as I was helped too. Elisa had started as a bouncer here before getting into social activism, and I'd once seen her rip the arm off a werebear.

Instead, though, Elisa said, "All right, I'll meet you in my office."

"You have an office here?" I asked, surprised.

Kali frowned. "I was forced to make certain accommodations to the Network in order to remain in business."

That troubled me. "Okay, lead the way. Stay out of trouble, guys."

"What trouble could we possibly get into here?" David asked.

"We'll be fine," Melissa said.

Elisha proceeded to lead me past a set of doors to the hallways behind the bar. The walls had once been covered in graffiti calling for the overthrow of the Council, slurs against the U.S. government, various swear words, and the numbers of local hookers. They'd all been painted over with a tasteful eggshell blue, which seemed a direct counter to the rest of The Razor. There were three or four open doors in the hall, revealing people counting money, a storage room for drugs, and an armory. It was a lot more professional-looking operation than before.

Elisha's office was right beside Kali's, and it was a good deal more sedate than I'd expected. There was a plain metal desk with a laptop on it, a pair of chairs, a filing cabinet, a metal safe against the back wall, and a wall covered with photos of the Network's deceased. She sat down in a courteous, businesslike manner. Even her gaze remained even.

Something was wrong.

"I'm sorry about what happened," I said, instantly realizing that was the worst sort of thing to say.

It didn't have the effect I expected. "You shouldn't be, Iraq. You were right. We blundered blindly into our conflict with the Mexicans like children. There were other conflicts after it, exactly like you described. We lost Tyrone, Linsha, Paige, Todd, Grax, and Suicide in the six months you were gone but still in the city limits. After you were exiled, a good half of the remaining Network crew quit."

I grimaced, remembering each of those supernaturals as a friend or acquaintance. "You did the best job you could."

"I did," Elisa said, her voice now accusatory. "Did you know?"

"Know?" I asked, hoping she hadn't learned the truth in the past two years.

Elisha had. "That the Network was funded by the Old Ones?"

It was like a kick in the gut. "Yeah, I found out from Fatimah a few weeks before. I hadn't believed her, but she'd talked about it like it was self-evident. They built the opposition so they could control its narrative. Some real Emperor Palpatine shit."

Elisha raised an eyebrow.

"Okay, I stand corrected, sometimes *Star Wars* is applicable even to the supernatural," I said. I didn't want to tell you because I worried it would destroy you."

"So, you just decided I'd be better off blindly running off a cliff."

I grimaced. "Er, no? I tried to get you to resist. I tried to—"

"You tried everything but the truth," Elisha said. "Were you spying on us?"

I don't know what compelled me to tell the truth. "Yes."

Elisha's eyes narrowed before becoming dissonantly serene. "It's all right. I've suspected for a while and have long since stopped blaming you."

I blinked. "You have?"

"Oh yes," Elisha said, getting up from her seat and going to her filing cabinet. "I won't lie to you—I was in a very dark place for a while, but my situation allowed me to examine just what I was fighting for and how much I needed to be willing to sacrifice in order to make substantive change to the Vampire Nation."

"Uh, good. I guess." I remembered then why I was here. "Listen,

Elisha, there's something you need to know. There's this kind of uber-vampire who is planning to kill every vampire in the city. He almost destroyed the Apophis tonight and may be working with both Theodore Eaton as well as members of your group. Hell, maybe even you. I know you wouldn't—"

"Does the voivode know? Is she coming with her bogatyrs to kill us all?" Elisha reached into the filing cabinet and removed a small tube I couldn't quite make out the precise shape of.

"No." I shook my head. "I protected you."

"Thank you," Elisha said, walking over to me.

Then she stabbed me through the heart with a steel stake.

CHAPTER THIRTEEN

As I told Melissa, stakes through the heart don't kill vampires. They do, however, ruin your evening.

"Fuck!" I tried to shout but I only ended up speaking in a tone little above a whisper.

"You broke my heart, Iraq," Elisha said, sitting on the desk. "So now I've broken yours."

I managed to choke out. "I'm not Fredo! If anyone, I'm Sonny!"

Elisha stared at me like I was insane. "You realize you're going to die now, right? Half of the people out there are my chosen followers. All of the weekend warriors and half-hearted members have been purged or abandoned the cause. What we have now is a collection of true believers who will join in the fight to purge the Old Ones from this city. Tonight."

She was probably right about me dying. I couldn't use my powers with a stake through my heart. Thoth said that was because the heart was where the Egyptians believed the soul rested and where witches believed all magic flowed. I believed it was just damned hard to use mental abilities when you had a goddamn piece of metal stabbing through you.

I couldn't even contact Melissa through our bond.

"Only half ... you're slipping," I managed to say through choked breaths. I needed to keep her talking. Not just because I didn't want to die, but because I actually wanted to know what the hell she was thinking.

Hadn't the previous failed attempts to fight the Old Ones taught her anything? The Vampire Nation wasn't a street gang; it was an undead superpower!

"We only need half with Renaud," Elisha said, sitting on the edge of her desk in front of me. "He's the most powerful vampire I've ever encountered. He's twice as old as the voivode and even more powerful, having absorbed the blood of many other vampires to give him their strength. You've not seen the things he can do or the miracles he can perform."

"Yay for vampire Jesus," I said, each syllable painful. "Are ... you ... insane?"

Elisha went back around her desk and pulled out a long, thick-handled Bowie knife. "You don't get it, do you, Iraq?"

"Stop calling me that."

Elisa shook her head. "You were right. We were playing a sucker's game. I was blind before, but now I see the strings. If we're ever to be free, the Young Bloods and other supernaturals, we have to kill the Old Ones. They may be immortal to most people, but weapons made from their bones can permanently destroy them."

Damn, Thoth wasn't going to be happy about that getting out.

"You can't win," I said, more pitying than anything else. I summoned all my strength to speak clearly and concisely. "This is another fight you're leading your people to slaughter in."

"I don't think so," Elisha said, coming back to me with the Bowie knife. "You haven't seen what he can do. All we have to do is eliminate the twenty richest vampires in the city along with their masters in the Council of Ancients. Their entire network of cash, blackmail, and graft will collapse. From there, the Vampire Nation will lose its grip on the Young Bloods and lesser supernaturals, making a more equitable society. It'll be like the American Revolution for our kind."

"More like ... the French," I said, wondering how she could be so naive. "Renaud wants to kill all vampires everywhere."

I wasn't so sure about that, honestly, but I was starting to see why everyone was sticking to that story if he inspired this kind of loyalty.

Elisa smiled beatifically. "Renaud loves me."

Oh my God, really? What was with this guy? Was every woman dying to get into his jaws? "You too?"

That was when Elisa's shoulders slumped and all fire left her for straight-up indignation. "What the hell do you mean, *you too*?"

I struggled not to say something that would get me killed. I failed. "Lisha, you got Twilighted."

"Fuck you, Stone!" Elisha shouted, kicking me in the chest and causing my chair to fall to the ground with a loud bang.

Seconds later, Melissa was inside the room. The super-fast vampire possessed super-hearing and had come immediately upon hearing the scuffle. Elisha scoffed at Melissa before swinging around a fist at her head with the force to knock it clean off. I could only watch in slow motion, unable to do a thing.

Melissa ducked, grabbed the stake in my chest, and then jabbed it into Elisha's chest. Elisha's mouth spit up blood as her eyes widened in shock. The Bowie knife in her hands dropped to the ground and rolled across the floor.

"I've staked a few vampires before," Melissa said, picking up the Bowie knife off the ground. "The trick is to take their heads after you do it. I prefer using a machete, but I suppose I can just saw your undead head clean—" She lifted up the knife to start cutting.

I grabbed her by the shoulder. "No, don't—"

"She was about to kill you," Melissa said. "Either because you were a shitty boyfriend or because she's a goddamn terrorist."

"Language, Sister Christian. What would the Lord say?"

"To kill all the bloodsucking abominations, but I'm still working that out thanks to my new condition."

I wasn't sure if she was joking or not. "Don't hurt her."

"Why?" Melissa said. "You love her?"

I made a *pfft* noise. "I think we're past that point. I will say, though, we're more likely to get out of here alive if she's not dead when they find her. She's got a lot of friends outside, and I don't want to be the one to rile them up."

"Screw you," Elisha said, her voice barely a whisper. "I'm not telling you anything."

"We need to get her laptop and what's in her safe," I said. "The password is her cat's name. She never changed the safe's default configuration."

Elisha let out a primal scream that sounded only like a series of unpleasant grunts.

Melissa pulled off her coat and put the laptop in its interior before starting to hack the safe. "What are we trying to do here?"

I felt my wounded heart start to heal. It was painful and made me hungry as hell. "We need to find out where they intend to hit the city's Old Ones."

"Do we really care?" Melissa asked a pertinent question. "They're kind of assholes."

"You have a point," I said, cursing. "But I owe Thoth. Besides, if the Old Ones are all killed, then Renaud wins, and he's a bigger asshole than all of them put together. Triggering a mass supernatural genocide isn't going to make the world a better place either. There's always going to be monsters, humans or otherwise, even if vampires are kind of on the far end of things."

"All right," Melissa said, opening the safe and revealing dozens of files as well as a couple of flash drives. She pulled them all out and put them on her coat, grabbing the edges and turning it into a makeshift sack.

Kali arrived at the doorway with David just behind her.

"Oh my goodness!" Kali said, which I'd heard her say before pulling out scimitars of light to slaughter people.

"It's not what it looks like," I said, trying to stand up.

"It looks like you got staked, then Melissa staked Elisha. Oh, and you're robbing the place," David said.

"See," I said, shaking my head. "Completely wrong. We were attacked by alien vampires and one of them was wearing a sexy string rubber-band thing. We're just cleaning out anything sensitive before she returns."

"Oh, I know her!" Kali said, trying to joke even as she was appalled. "You need to leave now, Pete. The people in the main hall aren't Network. They're a collection of some of the worst supernatural gangs in the Rust Belt. Elisha has brought them all in with the help of Eaton."

"Eaton?" I said, stunned. "She wouldn't work—"

"She staked you, man," David interrupted. "Screw her."

"You'll find him where no vampire will go in the city," Kali said, walking over to Elisha. "Now you have to get out of here before I remove Elisha's stake."

"What?" I said, both stunned and confused.

"Why would you do that?" Melissa asked.

"Because I have to live here," Kali said, her voice low. "I'm older than anyone outside the Council of Ancients. The important thing to stay alive as long as I have is to stay neutral in most conflicts."

"Those who sit on the fence tend to be kicked by both sides," I said, not envying her position. "Thank you, though."

"Good luck," Kali said. "You have a minute."

That was far less time than I was hoping she'd give me. I started immediately toward the door, struggling to ignore the smell of human blood from the servants in the other rooms. I wanted to rip out their throats and drink their life fluids. There were no animals nearby, and my companions were not enticing due to our bond, but everyone else was fair game.

Even vampires.

When Melissa and David passed me by, I shut the door and struggled to keep a level head. I hadn't been this hungry since my exile, since that night, and the very air seemed to have a taste to it. I clenched my fist before opening it over and over again, trying to distract myself from the Need. My fangs extended against my will, another sign I was losing control.

"Are you okay?" David asked, putting his hand on my shoulder.

"No," I said, pulling away. "Let's get out of here."

"Is there a back door?" Melissa asked.

"No. Just head out the front door."

I closed the door behind us, trying to act casual despite the fact that we were carrying a makeshift sack full of stolen files and a laptop. Oh, and my sweatshirt was torn open with blood on the edges, which was bound to attract attention from everyone of the fanged persuasion once we got out into the main hall of The Razor.

At least I knew where Eaton was.

"So, I just want to say it's been a very interesting night," Melissa said, walking alongside me down the hall. "I appreciate you taking the time to teach me about vampire weaknesses, help me kill a bunch of former friends turned evil, and all that. However, it occurs to me I might never want to see you again after tonight."

"Funny, because I thought we were going to pick out china patterns together."

"Ha ha," Melissa said.

"Listen, seriously, I get it. Undeath is hard, though, so if you ever need a friend then please give me a call. It's the major thing I hate about the supernatural world; everyone seems to be at each other's throats."

Melissa grimaced. "Sorry about that."

"That actually wasn't a reference to you. Still, please don't ever do that again." I wasn't about to tell her it had felt like pure heaven, pain, and a jolt of electricity to the brain all at once.

That would be weird.

"Well, I'm glad you two are getting along now," David said, frowning. "Pete—"

"Stone," I corrected. "Kali and Thoth can call me Peter. Because they scare me."

"Stone," David said, annoyed. "Can we talk about you mind-zapping me back at the Apophis? Because that was not cool."

The three of us arrived in the main hall of The Razor. Almost all of the other supernaturals were silent now and looking in our general direction. That was not a good sign.

"Later," I said to David. "Much later."

"I think you're right," David muttered.

Jumping Jack Flash lifted his mug. "From hell's heart did Melissa stab at me. For hate's sake, we spit my last at she."

A good half of the thugs present pulled out pistols, crossbows, swords, and bats with silver spikes, and one guy grew what looked to be Wolverine's claws.

"Damn," David said, surveying the main hall. "We've been 'Wrath of Khan-ed'!"

"That's from Moby Dick originally," Melissa corrected, staring forward in horror.

"Who gives a shit!" I shouted.

Dozens of guns fired in our direction all at once, enough to tear us to pieces. I focused on my desire NOT TO DIE and threw out my hands, hoping to God or the Devil or Dracula that I wasn't about to end my unlife in this crappy bar. Much to my surprise, it worked. I didn't know if the prayer did it or the sheer horror of the situation, but all of the bullets in the air started to move very slowly. They weren't stopped but they were moving at a glacial pace.

"Move it!" I shouted, grabbing David by the arm and dragging him along as I decided to go to the right to avoid the gunshots coming at me. It weirdly put me in mind of that final scene of Prometheus when the two survivors (both the hot women on the ship, go figure) ran forward as a gigantic doughnut tried to squash them. You know, never deciding to go left or right.

OK, I'd been watching way too much sci-fi on Fridays with David. This week was *Anaconda, Ride Along, XXX: State of the Union,* and any other cheesy Ice Cube movie I could Netflix.

David and I were about halfway down the main hall, Melissa zipping past us right to the doors (I hated super-speed as a power), when time resumed its normal flow. Gunfire smashed into the back of the bar, causing dozens of bottles to explode and pour onto the ground as we continued legging it like Usain Bolt to the front doors. Thankfully, the confusion meant we were right by Melissa by the time I heard some assholes pointing back to us. "They're at the end of the hall! Get 'em!"

Lacuna Coil's "Swamped" was playing on the jukebox while I lamented how I kept getting into these sorts of situations. Both Melissa and David were already out the bar's wooden doors when I started exiting, only to be shot twice in the back before a two-hundred-pound giant wolf landed on me. I stumbled out the door, obviously, while it shifted back into a naked human, its claws burying themselves into my shoulders while it bit my throat. That was when I lost control and let the werewolf know why it was a bad idea to try to outfang a vampire.

I sank my fangs into its jugular and ripped out a chunk of flesh, spitting it out before clamping my mouth down on the open wound. The blood from the werewolf's heart poured down my throat like a waterfall. It was the sweetest wine, the best sex, and the most amazing drug I'd ever taken all rolled into one.

Tears of blood welled in my eyes while I gulped down mouthful after mouthful of delicious blood. I'd kept myself abstinent on a diet of strict animal blood with only the occasional blood bags or corpse juice, but this? This was the true life of a vampire. I thought I could survive without ever doing this again, that the unnamed girl I'd killed would be the last, but it had been a fever dream.

This was glorious.

God help me.

As the creature died on top of me, I stood up and threw its

body like a ragdoll through the opening doors. It slammed into the gathering lynch mob beyond and knocked over fifteen of them like bowling pins. The resulting domino effect bought me enough time to run to the car even as I heard a window bust from a gunshot while David tried to start the car. I shook my head, weaving in a pattern I hoped would keep the snipers from getting a good shot before jumping through the busted driver's side window like the Dukes of Hazzard (not that I ever watched that show). I landed in the passenger's side before tossing the keys at David. The car peeled out seconds later.

"They're going to follow us!" David shouted. "They have motorcycles and I think one of those shots hit our back tire."

"They're not going to follow us!" Melissa shouted back.

"How do you know?" I said, calling back.

That was when a grenade thrown by Melissa exploded among the bikes, creating a fireball that stood out even in this neighborhood. The gang of thugs left behind soon disappeared, flat tire or no, with the sounds of a dozen cop cars coming toward The Razor. As distractions went, I suspected that one was in the Top Five I'd seen.

Climbing to my feet in the passenger's side, I looked back at her. "You know, Mel, for a vampire-hating bigot, I'm starting to like you."

CHAPTER FOURTEEN

Against all odds, we managed to get away from The Razor's thugs with some surprisingly adept automobile hide-and-seek by David. In the end, he managed to bring my damaged car to my cousin Paul's all-night garage. Paul was a human but didn't mind taking vampire money or temporarily switching out cars as long as I gave him what was left of the two thousand dollars Thoth had given me.

Easy come, easy go.

An hour later, we were on the road again in a modified 1990 claret Dodge Dakota which was somehow even shittier and more beat-up than the one I'd driven into Paul's garage riddled with bullet holes. Still, it was inconspicuous and allowed me to work on getting the next phase of our so-called plan working. Melissa was sitting in the back of the car and we were just driving around at this point, taking in the sight of Old Detroit as I tried to figure out the meaning of Kali's clue.

The last place in the city a vampire would go? What the hell did that mean? It didn't help that the majority of the buildings that were still open as we reached midnight were the ones that catered to the undead or were run by them. My least favorite were the numerous Cash for Blood buildings, predatory loan offices, and other places designed to take advantage of the city's desperate. I also saw a few Debt Redemption and Accrual Cancellation (or DRAC) offices which were a unique vampire twist on taking advantage of America's debt.

Prostitution was still illegal in Michigan, albeit barely enforced even in cities not making their living off vice, but selling your blood to vampires was most certainly not illegal and only twelve states had managed to pass ordinances against it. DRAC contracts agreed to have a mortal sell their blood to a vampire "on call" whenever they wanted for however long it would take to work off their debt. You could imagine how that was being exploited.

One of the few times I'd ever seen Thoth go against his fellow Old Ones was in opposing it. He'd been convinced it was a bad idea after a habitual gambler had attempted to sell him his wife, a local channel's weather girl, in exchange for saving their house. Thoth had ended up eating him and taking her on as a Bloodslave—which he seemed to think was heroic, but I found just as horrifying as if he'd just taken her outright. Either way, DRAC contracts were an accepted part of New Detroit society now. It made me think the HRL had a point.

"Any luck with hacking Elisha's laptop?" I asked.

"Is it hacking when you knew the password?" Melissa said, her feet up along the seat of the cramped back of the Dakota.

"That's actually how real hacking works," David clarified. "Before I dropped out of college, I used to get into people's bank accounts just by knowing their pets' names and asking them which street they grew up on."

"Uh-huh, and how did that work out?" I asked.

David frowned. "I got caught and was forced to drop out of college. Can we talk about you mind-zapping me again?"

I didn't have anything better to discuss. "Listen, David, I'm sorry about that. I am. However, if you mouthed off in front of the voivode then you'd probably get your ass murdered. I couldn't live with myself if that happened to you."

I was surprised to find out I meant it.

David couldn't meet my gaze. "I get that, I do, but it was still a shitty thing to do. You can't tell me you didn't enjoy it, either."

He was right, I had. "I promise I'll never do it again. It's a tempting power to use, but it's not right."

"You're damned right it's not," David said, showing surprising seriousness.

"Thank you for sticking by me despite it, though," I said.

That brought a smile to David's face. A serious expression then replaced it, but a different kind than the one he'd had previously. "I'm sorry you ended up breaking your fast, Pe—Stone."

I stared at the road, then shook my head. "Yeah, me too, but it was bound to happen eventually."

It was nice, actually, to have the taste of the werewolf blotting out the taste of the little girl I'd killed. I'd never even found out her name, never even wanted to know her name, but now the werewolf's blood was making her seem like a distant memory. I hated not being able to remember the taste anymore but also was grateful. Maybe this was something I could live with after all, as horrible as that was.

"You two are close," Melissa said, not looking up from her computers. "Like brothers."

"Yeah, like brothers," David said, disappointedly.

I pointedly chose to ignore that. "My question still stands."

"Yeah, I've had some luck," Melissa said, surprising me. "Apparently, Renaud was in contact with Elisha for some time—"

"Yeah, contact," I said, accenting the word. I was surprised I was jealous.

"Yeah, I saw that too," Melissa muttered, disgusted. "Some of the e-mails here are pretty spicy."

I snorted. "Anything useful?"

"Renaud's plan is two-fold," Melissa explained. "He was going to blow up the Apophis to make it look like a vampire civil war had gotten thousands of humans killed. He paid Eaton off to get all of his people past security by claiming he just wanted to murder Thoth. Renaud mentioned that Eaton very much wanted to take over the casino himself and figured he could persuade the voivode to let him have it."

"Oh that bastard," I muttered. "That should be my inheritance!"

"Way to show your sympathy, Stone," David said.

"Vampires don't usually leave wills," I said, "but I'm still in Thoth's."

Melissa continued. "After that, Eaton gave Renaud the location of a meeting place of Old Ones who were coming here to the city to discuss financial matters. Apparently, a whole lot of Old Ones, including several Ancients, will be present. Renaud intends to send the Network to attack them with him in the lead. They've got almost a hundred hardened killers with magic and superpowers on their side."

"It still sounds like suicide," I said, unimpressed with their plan. "Thoth is the weakest of the Old Ones and could kick that entire bar's ass."

"Elisha brings that up, but Renaud says he has a plan," Melissa said, shrugging. "There's a lot of information in these files about chemical compositions, blood types, and some scientific reports, but it's all Greek to me."

"We'll fax it to Thoth and Fatimah's people at the Apophis," I said, trying to remember if there was an all-night photocopier place in the area.

"Why not just phone them?"

I frowned. "I tried back at Paul's. Thoth is off trying to get in touch with the City Court to discuss what's been going on. If there's a big meeting with the Vampire Nation's leaders, then he'll probably be there. They don't allow cell phones during those."

"Cell phones bother Old Ones?" David asked.

"Yeah, they're always worried about insider trading or information being recorded," I said, being quite serious. "You don't get to be a billionaire unless you're paranoid as fuck. It's why vampires are such good businessmen."

David, thankfully, didn't point out the obvious about me being a shitty one. "So after we do that, what do we do?"

"We find Eaton and get him to fess up," I said. "It won't do jack to improve our situation with Renaud, but it'll result in his getting brought up and probably executed. I don't want him escaping the city and ending up in Paris for a decade until the heat dies down."

"Like you did?" David asked.

"The outskirts of town aren't Paris," I said, regretting the fact I needed to stay so near my home soul. Maybe if I brought a few jars of dirt with me.

The thought of being able to drag Eaton before the City Court and the voivode being unable to do anything about it was pretty sweet. I imagined the next *bellidux* wouldn't be much better, as they'd probably just promote one of Eaton's creations or buddies, but it would still be a small bit of justice for a town that had suffered under that son of a bitch for a long time. It would be a small bit of justice for that girl I'd ... we'd murdered.

"Sounds like a plan," Melissa said.

I had to ask something. "So, what really motivated you to turn on Renaud?"

"Excuse me?" Melissa looked up. "Finding out he was a terrorist isn't enough for you?"

"Maybe," I said, still trying to get my measure of her. "The thing is, Renaud could have fed you his blood and mind-zapped you. Hell, he's probably strong enough to mind-zap you as is."

Melissa twitched and I realized I should probably drop the subject. After all, once you started thinking about vampires being able to control your mind, you started getting paranoid about what was actually your choice and what wasn't. I'd occasionally wondered if the reason I loved Thoth the way I did was because the old bastard made me do it. The thing was, if he was doing that, would I ever question it? So was it legitimate? Or was he so intelligent that he allowed me just enough leash so that I never thought about it? Those were the kind of thoughts I had about a vampire I liked. Now those thoughts were there for an avowed vampire hater who had gone and gotten romantically involved with one? Because, unlike in the movies, the majority of times someone did an about-face like that, it was because they had been hypnotized into becoming a vampire's loyal blood whore.

"Your point?" Melissa said, her voice cold and unfeeling. Clearly, she was thinking the same thing now.

"If you were able to go against him like that," I said, backtracking, "you had to have some sort of motivation other than just a bunch of generic people being endangered. You needed something personal to motivate you. I mean, vampires killed your family."

"Not all of them," Melissa said.

"What?" I asked.

"My brother Jim is alive, sort of," Melissa said.

I paused. "You have a brother named Jim Morris? Did your parents hate him?"

Melissa took a deep breath. "They did eventually when he came out."

"You're really not convincing me you're the good guy in all this," David said, looking back at her.

"How did your parents react when you said you liked to screw guys?" I asked.

"They'd known since I was thirteen," David asked, glancing over at me. "They were more annoyed when I cheated on my boyfriend with the girl next door. They'd been so proud of having a gay son that bi just seemed like a step back."

I actually laughed at that, which I shouldn't have. "So Minister Morris kicked out your brother before vampires killed him for being part of the HRL. Did you ever find your brother again?"

"He was disowned when I was thirteen," Melissa said. "I didn't think to look him up until much later. It was Renaud, in fact, who inspired me to do it. That's when I found out he was a vampire too."

Melissa let out a gallows laugh.

"What's so funny?"

"*He's a cancer doctor,*" Melissa said, looking close to tears. "He uses blood so he can help them survive more chemotherapy and to hypnotize them into not feeling pain. He and his partner are among the nicest people I've ever met. They're thinking about adopting some special needs children."

"Prejudice is a bitch," I said. "So that's when you started thinking this whole vampire hunting thing was a lost cause."

"I'd started thinking it a long time ago. I was willing to go along with it until then, though. I'm just sorry it took me until this point to change my mind."

Nobody said anything after that, right up until we passed a Burgertown. Seeing the White Castle-looking building with its cheerful hamburger sign, I immediately hit the brakes and would have gotten us into an accident if there had been anyone behind us. It was rare I had eureka moments in real life, but this was one of them.

"What the hell, Pete?" David asked. "Are you high? Does werewolf blood work like meth?"

"More like pot," I said, shrugging. "Slight sense of euphoria. It's the only drug I used while alive, anyway, and purely for coping with my wartime experiences."

"Uh-huh," David said.

I smiled. "Burgertown is the safest place for anyone to hide out from a vampire."

"What?" Melissa and David said simultaneously.

I did a U-turn and pulled the car into the fast food joint's parking lot. "Everyone knows about the sunlight, stake through the heart, fire, and decapitation stuff. Three out of four of those will kill a human, so it's fine. However, when you're really young, you have a lot of incredibly annoying minor weaknesses no one tells you about. Most of these you'll grow out of while some get worse, but they're irritating as fuck."

I hadn't told Melissa about all of our weaknesses. I'd told her about the big ones, mind you, but not the smaller ones. The ones that afflicted vampires until they were old enough to ignore them but still came up in day-to-day life. The kind of things that were more effective than laying huge crosses on your door or buying a flamethrower.

Melissa looked genuinely interested. "Like what?"

"Counting sesame seeds."

Melissa and David exchanged a look.

"You're kidding," Melissa said.

"I wish I was," I said, grumbling. "One time I was visiting an old friend here and I ended up spending an hour picking every single seed out of his burger."

"So all vampires are OCD?" Melissa blinked.

"Only about sesame seeds," I answered.

Melissa scrunched her brow. "How does that even make sense as a weakness?"

"I don't know!" I said, parking the car. "Best of all, I don't have to. I only have to know Eaton is here."

"Why this Burgertown?" David asked. "Hell, why Burgertown in general?"

"They produce the Super-Sesame Seed Bun Combo," I said, shaking my head. "It's on pictures, it's on display, and there are usually full display cases of freshly made buns in order to show they're fresh. It's like an irresistible command to go over them all. As for why this Burgertown, I heard an Old One actually works here. A guy who doesn't mind the atmosphere and runs a side business smuggling supernaturals out of the city. I never came back here after the first time, so I don't know him, but it's the best lead we have."

"It's a pretty poor lead," Melissa said. "Are you sure we'll be able to go in?"

I nodded. "As long as I keep my eyes off the things, I should be fine. There's also a pair of cheap-ass sunglasses in the glove compartment. I checked when looking at the registration. That should help. You might want to stay in the car."

"Fat chance of that," Melissa said.

"Well, if you're immune to crosses and saying the Lord's name, maybe you're immune to this too," I said, hoping that wasn't the case. Melissa had already hit the lottery of vampirism and I was hoping she didn't get anything else before she'd earned it.

Me, petty? No!

The three of us started to get out. There was a feeling of excitement in the air as well as newfound purpose.

David then ruined the mood. "Wait, does this mean the Count of Sesame Street is accurate vampire lore?"

I paused by the car door. "I never thought about it like that."

"Mind blown," David said, holding out his hands in front of him.

"Any other weaknesses I should know about?" Melissa asked, looking away from Burgertown as if she'd caught a glimpse of something she shouldn't have.

"Well, you know about the verbena thing, but it's just about everything that can really fuck up your day. I still live in Detroit in part because whenever I go outside the city, I can't sleep unless I have a jar full of dirt. I hate going outside during rainstorms because of all the storm drains, and crossing rivers is a phobia I'm working on. The missing reflection thing is something you gain as you grow older. Oh, and you don't have to invite me in, but if I'm not invited then I can't use my powers inside the building."

"Wow, that sucks," David said. "No wonder so many vampires commit suicide."

"Yes, it's that versus all-consuming guilt over the violence of the lifestyle," Melissa snapped back.

"No, David's right," I corrected him, thinking about the girl I'd killed. "You have to force yourself to remember the guilt."

"What about garlic?" Melissa asked.

I paused. "Weird. You know that's actually the *one thing* that doesn't seem to affect us. I was kind of disappointed, to be honest, as I've never been a big Italian sort of guy."

"Huh," Melissa said, processing all this. "Wait, does the running water thing mean vampires can't take showers?"

"I'm strictly a bath man," I said, getting the sunglasses in the glove compartment and putting them on. "Now let's go get us a lawman."

CHAPTER FIFTEEN

Even though I was wearing a pair of sunglasses, the sight of the Burgertown's interior caused every hair on the back on my neck to stand up. I had to focus entirely forward on the checkout counter to avoid having my attention drawn to the pictures of sesame seed buns on the wall as well as the display case of actual buns. Buns full of sesame seeds. Beautiful, enchanting, tiny, perfect sesame seeds.

1 …

2 …

3 …

No, I am not doing this! I am not a number; I am a free man! This is a stupid weakness, even worse than garlic, and I don't know why the hell vampires have it! Goddammit, at least fire and decapitation are badass!

"How you holding up?" I asked, having stepped one foot into the room.

"Hmm?" Melissa said. "No problems whatsoever."

"Really?" I said, having unconsciously placed my hand on her shoulder for support.

"Nope." Melissa looked around. "I'm wondering about what it'll be like to never eat meat again. But I hated Burgertown, so there's no problem."

"What?" I asked, distracted from the compulsion. "Everyone loves Burgertown. They're the best hamburger chain in the Rust Belt."

"Not me," Melissa said. "I only ordered fries whenever my father insisted we eat here."

"Heathen," I said, so shocked by her blasphemy against the one food I would miss from my mortal days. "David?"

"Yeah?" David asked, looking uncomfortable.

"I need you to wait outside," I said, looking for some sign of the Old One who supposedly ran this place. Right now, there was only a human guy in a paper hat eating french fries at the counter. The rest of the restaurant was empty and I was glad of that. If Eaton was here, I fully expected things to get bloody—and in a non-vamp-appealing way.

"Why?" David asked, confused.

"Because I need you to watch to make sure no one goes out the back door," I said, actually wanting him out of the way because I was afraid he'd get murdered in any conflict involving me and the undead.

"All right," David said, frowning. "But only because you asked me to."

I handed him the car keys, just in case he had to give chase.

"Eaton is here," Melissa said, interrupting our little get-together.

"What?" I looked around and accidentally caught a glimpse of way too many sesame seeds. I didn't need to count them, but they gave me a monstrous migraine.

"In the back," Melissa said, pointing to the kitchen doors. "I can hear his voice. He's talking to a guy who sounds like the movie Dracula."

"Lugosi, Lee, Langella, Oldman, or Butler?"

"Gerard Butler played Dracula?" Melissa asked.

"Yeah, *Dracula 2000*. I didn't recognize him the first time I saw it," I said, remembering how awful that movie was.

"No, I mean he sounds like the thick-European-accented Lugosi kind."

"Mel, no real vampire actually sounds like—"

That was when I was proven wrong. "Welcome to Burgertown! May your time here be as fruitful as a productive peasant's harvest. Ha ha ha ha."

I lowered my sunglasses to the bridge of my nose, then turned to see where the heavily-accented Slavic voice was coming from.

Standing outside the kitchen doors was a five-foot-six man with a widow's peak and graying black hair who actually resembled Bela Lugosi to a certain extent. The old, sad, underpaid, overworked Bela Lugosi who worked for Ed Wood until his dying day.

He wasn't wearing a cape and a tuxedo—that would have been a bridge too far—but he was wearing a black sports jacket and a button-down shirt with black jeans. Like he couldn't afford even a cheap business suit but wanted to look like a half approximation. It was doubly weird because his hands were covered in gold and jeweled rings that were probably worth more than my house.

The worst part? This guy was the real deal. I could feel it from across the room that not only was he a vampire, but he was a powerful one too. A genuine Old One who could probably put three to four hundred years to his name at the least. His dry papery skin and elongated fingernails also marked him as one of the older, "purer" strains of vampirism from Eastern Europe or Egypt, which had an advantage over the more human-looking modern ones.

And he was working at a fast food joint.

Burgertown.

I stared at the sight. "Are you shitting me?"

"I shit you not," the Old One said. "Burgertown is always open to cater to those with discriminating tastes in hamburger buns."

"But not meat," Melissa whispered.

"What was that?" the Old One asked.

"Nothing," Melissa said. "Nice to meet you, Mister—"

"Graff Yorga of the House Basarab," the Old One said cheerfully. "Can I take your order?"

"Graff?" Melissa asked, walking up to the counter.

David proceeded to leave, looking embarrassed.

I followed Melissa, torn between my desire to go after Eaton and my confusion over what the hell a vampire this old was doing working here for minimum wage. It had to be a scam, right? Old Ones, at least, always had money.

Yorga was too busy answering Melissa's question to pay me much heed, though. "Well, it's kind of like Prince. I didn't have the title while I was alive, but since I outlived all my brothers and their descendants, I don't think they'll mind. As for the rest, my lineage is very famous, which isn't always a good thing when you're a vampire. Back in the Old Country, living in castles and having titles is just how things are done. Here, in America, it's like you're some kind of joke. Very distressing."

"Because of Drac—"

"Don't mention his name," Yorga hissed. "Mister 'I'm so famous,

I'm too cool for my family.' That's what you say now, cool, yes?"

"Yeah," I said, unable to take my eyes off the guy.

"I had some movies named after me," Yorga said, frowning. "But do people remember them? No!"

"I remember them," the guy eating fries beside him said.

"Shut up, mortal," Yorga said. "And I really need you to order something."

"I'll have the large Coca-Cola," I said. "I can't swallow it, but I like to swish it around in my mouth."

Yorga smiled. "Thank you. Please feel free to keep talking. I so rarely get to discuss things like this."

Wow, this was surreal. Was this how I looked to the outside world? "How did you end up working here?"

This was blowing a lot of my presuppositions about the way things were supposed to work out of the water. It was one thing for the majority of vampires to be poor. It was dead wrong and shouldn't be the case, but I'd been prepared for it by the trashy vampires of *Near Dark,* John Carpenter's *Vampires,* plus *30 Days of Night.* But Old Ones? Old Ones were supposed to be above this shit. Also, man, he really needed to modernize his dress sense. This was America. Okay, now I was being racist and classist. I needed to tone down that shit and listen.

Yorga gave an embarrassed shrug. "One day you're ruling eleven villages who send their sons and daughters to stay with you for a year on their eighteenth birthday, the next the communists have tanks rolling up on your palace to shell it to the ground."

"Uh-huh," I said, speechless.

Yorga clenched a fist. "Fuck communism. I wish I'd made Reagan into a vampire. He's a true hero for defeating the Red Menace."

I mentally contacted David. *Please tell me I'm not this bad.*

This guy? David asked, hopefully still watching the backdoor. *Not this bad. Close, but not this bad.*

"I think Reagan was an awful president," the guy eating fries said, looking even more bored than David was at his job.

Yorga turned to him and waved his bony fingers. "Maggots, you're eating maggots."

"Doesn't work on me," the guy eating fries said, getting up and walking to the kitchen.

"Ugh," Count Yorga said. "This is what happens when an Old One doesn't have the proper lifestyle. You can't even pull off simple party tricks."

"I'm sorry," I said, half sincere.

Yorga continued rambling. "You know Kiefer Sutherland is a vampire now? My cousin Vassily offered to make him one after the Bailout."

"Are you sure that's true?" I asked, trying to see inside the kitchen as the doors flipped open. "Because Hollywood loves cultivating rumors about that shit. California's laws are so draconian about privacy that anyone or everyone could be a supernatural."

Yorga started entering the code for my Coca-Cola. "Well, I know what Vasilly tells me, and he works at one of the studios. Tom Cruise is definitely a vampire."

I snorted. "Oh, like that surprises anyone."

"How about Brad and Angie?" Melissa piped in, not helping matters. We didn't need to be dealing with this fruit loop.

"I heard he was up for the offer, but she turned it down," Yorga said, holding his hand out for the cash. "Werepanther."

I passed him my debit card inside. I wasn't going to trust him with any more of my rapidly diminishing cash.

"No!" Melissa gasped. "She didn't want to be an immortal werepanther?"

Yorga snorted. "No, you can't combine things. Screw that *Underworld* bullshit."

"You know the next seasons of *The Bachelor* and *The Bachelorette* are going to be vamp themed," Melissa said.

"Really?" Yorga said. "That seems like a bad idea."

"Why?"

"I mean, unless it's all vampires, some of the cast are going to get eaten," Yorga said. "Or changed or made into slaves. That's just how these things go."

"Better for ratings, I guess," I said, tiring of this conversation.

David contacted me. *Still no sign of Eaton, Boss. If he's in there, he's waiting you out.*

Dammit, I thought back.

I'd actually been hoping Eaton would make a break for it. This was going to make things awkward. Even if Yorga was more Count Chocula than Vlad the Impaler, he was still an Old One and could tear me a new one if I pissed him off. Also, I wasn't entirely sold on this all being his real personality. All Old Ones were crafty sonsabitches, and not all of them were prideful.

The dude could just be acting like a Dracula Expy in order to get people to lower their guard. Let's face it, I was here because I suspected he was running a business smuggling vampires out of the city. Which meant he was willing to challenge the voivode and defy the Vampire Nation's laws.

"What's it like to live for centuries?" Melissa asked.

"Tiring," Yorga said, chuckling. "Honestly, it's wonderful. I don't get all of these younger vampires who keep complaining about their condition. In my day, you were lucky to live to thirty and if you did, you looked fifty. The very fact you don't have to use the bathroom anymore strikes me as something every vampire should be grateful for."

"I hadn't thought of that," Melissa said, blinking. "Ever?"

"Nope!" Yorga said. "We also—"

I decided to screw the pleasant chit-chat. "We need to speak with Eaton. Now."

Yorga narrowed his eyes. "Eaton? I don't know what you mean."

I frowned, adjusting my sunglasses so they covered my eyes completely. "Cut the crap, Yorga. We know you're harboring him like you've done so many others over the years. He's fucked up his position in the city and we need to—"

That was when he grabbed me by the throat and smashed me through the countertop.

"Jesus!" Melissa shouted, falling backward.

Yorga reacted like he'd had an air horn blown right next to his ears. He stopped smashing me up to cover his ears. He then grabbed me by the sweatshirt, lifting me up and hissing at me.

"Who sent you!?"

His hair had gone from graying to pure jet-black, and his irises were a brilliant shade of red. He looked about twenty years younger, and an aura of power and terrifying majesty surrounded him, putting to lie his earlier appearance.

"The voivode," I choked out. "She sent me."

"Liar!" Yorga shouted, hurling me across the Burgertown dining area and slamming me into a pair of tables. "It was Ashura who paid me. Gave me the go-ahead to smuggle him out so he could avoid the sun."

Dammit, that was something I should have expected. Ashura had been covering for her child for years. Why should a measly terrorist attack be any different? That didn't increase my chances of getting out of there alive, though.

Yorga climbed over the countertop and grabbed Melissa by the neck, throwing her over his shoulder into the soda fountain. That inspired me to get up, pull out my pistols, and start firing into Yorga.

They might as well have been squirt guns.

"Now you are going to tell me who sent you before I rip your head clean off!" Yorga said, walking forward with a slow, deliberate executioner's grace.

David mentally contacted me. *Eaton is making a run for it!*

Now is not the time!

I'm going after him!

No!

I was terrified for David, but I didn't have any options as Yorga was already upon me, ready to make good on his threat. "I'll talk, I'll talk!"

My attempts to buy time (HA!) for my time powers to kick in didn't do much good. Yorga raised me up by my throat. Two long claws popped out from his index and middle fingers as he raised them back to impale me through the eyes. It wasn't ripping my head clean off, but maybe he was saving that for later.

"Who is—" Yorga didn't get to finish because Melissa placed two straws crossed together against his face and started saying the Lord's Prayer. Okay, that was never going to work even if it was causing my head to hurt. Then Yorga's face caught fire.

"Argh!" Yorga shrieked, dropping me and holding his flaming face while the straws melted in the cross-shaped brand she'd created on his face.

"OK, that's an extreme reaction even by our standards," I said, climbing to my feet.

"Shoot him!" Melissa shouted, looking for another possible weapon to use against him.

That was when I reached into my jean pocket and pulled out the bone dagger Thoth had given me. I didn't actually want to kill Yorga, as that was crossing the Rubicon when you were undead.

Maybe it was a double standard that I now worried about killing my fellow bloodsuckers more than humans, but it was how I felt now. Either that, or I was thinking any man who tried to do the maggot joke couldn't be all bad.

So I just cut him across the arm with it. Sure enough, the wound caused him to shriek again before I held the dagger to his throat. "This can kill you forever, Old One. Get out of here and leave Eaton to me."

The hideous skinless burned face of Yorga turned to me, his eyes regenerating where everything else most certainly was not. The look he passed me was one of pure hatred. Hissing, he looked at his arm, then—I shit you not—turned into a fruit bat before flying out the glass wall of the Burgertown behind me. By the way, you may ask why fruit bat and not vampire bat? Well, the answer is fruit bats are *fucking huge.*

I stared, not quite sure what had happened. "Did we win?"

Melissa nodded. "Yeah."

That was when I noticed a sesame seed-covered hamburger bun on the ground and had to pick it up. "That's great. We should go make sure David is alive."

1 …

2 …

3 …

Melissa slapped it out of my hands.

CHAPTER SIXTEEN

I stumbled out of the Burgertown, hoping David was all right. The two of us had known each other for seven years and had a brief friendship during high school before his family had moved to a better part of town. I tried to contact him mentally, but my head was still ringing from where it had been pounded repeatedly against the ground.

My wounds had already healed, though, thanks to the potent blood in my veins. Werewolf blood was more nourishing, more powerful, and I felt stronger for having drunk it. I hoped—and it surprised me to think this—that Eaton had gotten away, because I'd prefer to let go the man I hated most than let David chase him down and get killed.

Not that I was going to tell David that.

Much to my surprise, I saw the parking lot contained a wreck with my cousin's Dodge Dakota smashed into the side of a cherry-colored SUV and the figure of Theodore Eaton trapped in between. David was standing in front of the sight, chuckling to himself and looking at the paralyzed vampire. Apparently, a piece of metal must have buried itself into Eaton's heart during the car wreck. Either that or he'd just been so smashed to pieces that he hadn't been able to regenerate.

"Booyah!" David said, sticking his fingers in the air with V signs. "Who's the man?"

I ignored him and stared at Eaton. The incapacitated vampire's face was contorted into a display of agony, his fangs on full display and sweat pouring down his face. Unlike what you'd see in some movies, vampires still had some non-bloody fluids running through them. Not the ones that most mattered, mind you, and I've got to tell you that was a real shock the first time I had sex post-creation.

Seeing Eaton helpless before me, though, drove out all of those quirky little observations. Instead, all I could feel was a kind of sadistic joy at the son of a bitch's state. I could imagine dragging him back to my trailer and burning away little bits of him in the sun for years. I wanted to pluck out his eyeballs, set them on fire, and make him hear as they burned nearby. I wanted to reach over and—

"Jesus Christ," David said. "That's cold-blooded shit."

"Ow!" I said, grimacing. "Don't say that!"

"Don't project your *Saw* fantasies in my head!" David replied. "I was never fond of the torture porn genre, especially when *Hostel* made me too scared to go on a European vacation and thus miss my chance to have sex with everyone willing to sleep with the horny American."

"I was kidding," I said, trying to explain my violent thoughts away.

"You really weren't."

"We need to get out of here," Melissa said, looking around at the sky for flying bats.

"I don't think Yorga is coming back," I said.

"The police then?"

"In Old Detroit? Why, did someone offer them a bribe to come by?"

Melissa rolled her eyes. "You're terrible."

"I'm sorry," I said, grinning from ear to ear. "This is just … so perfect."

Eaton made a couple of noncommittal grunts. He then muttered something that resembled a racial epithet.

"I'm sorry, what was that?" I said, cupping my hand to my ear. "I couldn't hear that over all the *schadenfreude*."

Eaton clenched his teeth. "I called you a worthless n—"

I climbed on top of the car hood, crouched down, grabbed him by the face, and placed my thumbs on his eyes. "I dare you to finish that sentence."

He did.

I started pushing his eyes into the back of his head.

"Peter!" Melissa shouted.

"He deserves worse!" I hissed. "You don't know what he's done."

"Torture isn't the way," Melissa said.

"He put an eight-year-old girl in front of me after starving me for a week."

Melissa blinked. "Kill that son of a bitch."

"Thank you!" I said, trying to figure out what way to do it. I didn't know if I could rip his head clean off, but it was certainly worth trying.

"You need this guy," David said, looking uncomfortable. "Alive. Unalive. In one piece. However you want to phrase it. Otherwise, you're going to probably be in trouble with the voivode for killing her child."

Dammit. Why the hell did I have such a politically apt servant? "Yeah, I suppose you're right. What they'll do to him is far worse than I could ever think of. You're about to get fucked, Eaton, with no Vaseline."

Like I said, torture wasn't really something vampires did during interrogations. Torture was done as a method of punishment. It was used as a "scare you straight" example the way the death penalty was, but a lot more effective, as executions were done in secret among humans but as sunburnt flayed bodies among the undead. I let go of Eaton, very reluctantly, before slapping him with the back of my hand.

Eaton hissed at my face, spitting a bit of blood at me and getting my pants legs. It was about the worst insult you could do among the undead since it was the equivalent of saying you weren't worth drinking from. "I'm protected, Stone. Ashura is the one who created me and once named me above all her other children. I'll be out in a few months."

I stepped down off the hood. "You were running, Eaton. Also, you tried to blow up the Apophis."

"I didn't know—"

"Yeah, you were only trying to help Renaud kill Thoth. You might have gotten away with just that, but Renaud was running the show and everyone is terrified of him according to what I've heard. Also, he did try to blow up the Apophis and that affects a lot of Ancients' bank accounts. They're not going to be forgiving that, and Ashura isn't going to be able to protect you. Besides, I've seen her other children. They all look like sexy movie vampires, and you've let yourself go this past century. You're done."

Surprisingly, Eaton was silent.

"Are you sure he's not going to get away with this?" Melissa asked. "Because we can cover him in gasoline and burn him right now. We also have that dagger of yours if you want to stab him enough times. There's also that enchanted shotgun in the back. Decapitation works well on vampires. Does it count if you blow their heads clean off?"

I stared back at her. "Damn girl, you've got a serious bipolar thing going on here. Are you for or against torture?"

"I'm against torture, unless they're evil psychopath sonsofbitches."

"I'm against torture, period," David said. "But we need to know everything we can if we're to prevent further destruction. I'm thinking when you turn me I can become a vampire detective."

I looked back at David. "You're no Hannibal King, David."

"Ryan Reynolds?" David said, confused. "No, I meant more like Angel."

"Hannibal King was the first vampire detective in the *Tomb of Dracula* comic," I explained. "That's actually where Blade first showed up. You know he was British originally? Idris Elba should have been him for maximum faithfulness, but that's not to put down Snipes because Snipes is God."

"And you complain about my geekiness."

"There's nothing geeky about comics," I said defensively. "Just sci-fi movies. *Star Wars* exempted because everyone loves *Star Wars*."

"Is Billie Dee Williams a vampire? My mom might have liked them if he was."

"Not that I know of. You want to go make him one?"

"Yes, please. Will Smith too."

"Hell no on Will Smith. I'm not going to ruin my chances with other black vampire women. I have enough trouble with Thoth around."

Melissa shrugged. "We could do Jada as well."

"Now you're talking."

"That is such bullshit!" David said, appalled at Melissa asserting his position. "You just don't want to admit you like the same kind of movies I do."

"You're right. I will never admit it."

"By the Elder Gods!" Eaton shouted, choking on his own words. "I'll tell you anything you want to know ... if you'll just ... shut ... up!"

Huh, interrogation by annoyance. I'd have to write that one down for later.

"Why did you do it?" David asked, staring at Eaton in confusion.

"I don't talk to bloodslaves," Eaton said, choking a bit before trying to raise a hand up to move the car in front of him. He couldn't do it. "I'll only answer to the vampires."

"You'll answer or we'll discuss the ins and outs of *Blacula*," I said, smiling. "I, for one, would love to see a remake with Jamie Foxx as Prince Mamuwalde. They could do a whole *Coming to America* thing with him looking for his bride in Queens."

"I'd rather you torch me and leave me for the sun." Eaton slumped his shoulders. "Ask your questions."

"Did you really do all of this for money?" David asked. "I mean, you're a vampire and have one of the richest in the world as your creator."

"You act like money ... isn't the most important thing to ... vampires." Eaton actually looked depressed. "I was once one of the richest men in Georgia and a patron of the arts."

"He's a slave owner too?" Melissa asked. "Stone, please, tear this bastard's head off."

"No slaves," Eaton said, choking. "I owned a rifle manufacturing plant and had paid employees. You can understand why we didn't want anyone near those who weren't of the right sort."

I walked over and slammed the back of my fist in his face, breaking his nose. It didn't heal, which meant he was low on blood.

Eaton took a deep breath. "I survived the Civil War and the Great Stock Market Crash but kept coming back to Ashura with my hat in my hand. When the Bailout happened, I couldn't donate shit to the fund because everything I had was in that bastard Madoff's fund."

For some reason, I found that outrageously funny. "Weren't vampires beneficiaries of that fund?"

"Shut up!" Eaton hissed.

"So, you betrayed Thoth for cash."

"I owed him up to my ... ass ... bastard. He let me win a lot of money at the casino after your exile and then I got cocky before he wiped out what few assets I had left. I needed to rebuild what I'd had before ... if I was ... to live the life to which I was accustomed."

I stared at him. "Yeah, well, you realize Renaud is going to attack the oldest vampires in the city, right? He's going to use the Network to help him slaughter some kind of meeting."

"Shit," Eaton said, actually looking concerned. "You've got to release me and get me to the City Council."

"One of those is happening," I said. "The other? Not so much."

Eaton was so furious his fangs jutted out, and he had to stop in order to retract them. Just as many actors had found out, it was hard to talk with fangs. You sounded like Sylvester the Cat and that totally destroyed any credibility you had as an undead fiend.

"I didn't know about the second attack," Eaton said, staring at them. "The Network is involved with Renaud too?"

"Nothing gets by you, chief, does it?" I said. "Or everything does. You sold the Network information on the meeting."

"I didn't know Renaud was involved!" Eaton hissed, sheer panic removing any of the hesitation his being staked would have normally caused. "I only found out about it when you mentioned it. He's involved with the Network. If he's actually behind all this, the Network's planned attack on the meeting won't just be a slaughter. He has the power to potentially kill them all!"

"OK, what meeting, first," I said.

"Walpurgis Night," Eaton said, as if it should mean anything to me. "It's tomorrow evening, when the Ancients send their representatives to the major cities of the New World in order to collect tithes and talk about upcoming business."

"Ah, tax day," I said, nodding. "Makes sense to be in April."

"Shut up and listen," Eaton said, his voice almost a whisper. "This is going to be a special meeting because almost all of the New World representatives are going to be in New Detroit. They're here to discuss how to keep the bankruptcy of the Vampire Nation a secret."

"Wait, what?"

Eaton rolled his eyes. "Did you really think vampires had enough money to keep the United States going? It's all smoke, hypnosis, and bank fraud. As long as they keep it going, though, they can milk the teat until they're rich again."

I stared at him. "God damn, my respect for the Vampire Nation just went up."

"It did?" Melissa said, appalled.

"Don't hate the player, hate the game."

Melissa shook her head. "I hated when guys told me that in college. I don't think it's any more appropriate now, especially when it risks the whole of the United States economy."

"Yeah, because that was in such good shape before," I said.

"Because the vampires wrecked it in the first place," Melissa replied.

"That's like saying the Illuminati are real and little green men! Or the moon landing was faked! It's a conspiracy theory!" I was appalled she believed that bullshit.

"Like vampires are secretly—" Melissa started to say.

"Could we focus on the ambush!" Eaton shouted, black blood drooling out of his mouth. "If Renaud leads his people to the conference, it could kill half of the Vampire Nation's leadership! Our entire ruling body would collapse overnight."

I shrugged. "Don't overstate matters, Eaton."

"Overstate matters?" Eaton said, appalled. "Do you understand what's at stake?"

"Renaud hasn't exactly wowed me with his Magnificent Bastardry™ if you catch my drift. Blowing up the Apophis would have worked if he hadn't changed Melissa and thus given us a warning it was going to happen. Then he left the Human Rights League people aware of the connection to the Network, which was followed up on. His operational security is shit and as soon as I tell the voivode about the coming attack, it's going to be moved."

"Well then, I had best make sure you don't tell them, shouldn't I?" I heard a thick, generic European-accented baritone voice behind me.

A cold chill passed over me as I turned around and saw the figure of Renaud standing behind me. My earlier description of a redheaded Kurgan was pretty accurate, though he was better-looking than Clancy Brown (no offense, Clancy) with softer features than in Melissa's vision.

If I had to give a weird description, it was like someone had grafted Kurt Cobain's head onto the Kurgan's body. I wondered if that was an illusion like some older vampires created, making themselves better looking to avoid being treated like they were sixteen or missing teeth like they were in life. Melissa, certainly, remembered him differently.

Standing beside him was the french-fry-eating fast food clerk who was holding a cellphone in his hand. I stared at him, stunned by the fact that I'd completely forgotten about him as well by the fact that he was a mole of Renaud's.

"Bastard," Melissa hissed at him, pulling out a grenade she'd hidden in her blouse.

"Drop it," Renaud commanded.

Melissa did, thankfully not having removed the pin yet.

Eaton started screaming for help.

David just stared at the vampire knight.

"What are you going to do?" I asked, trying to figure out a way to deal with this guy, given David had just wrecked our car and running would just mean we died tired. Even Melissa's super-speed couldn't help us. I tried to use my time powers, but of course, they didn't work. That would have been too easy.

"This," Renaud said, chuckling. There was a brief shuffle and in less than the blink of an eye he was holding Eaton's severed head in his hands. Blood dripped from the bottom of the man's neck before he dropped it on the ground. I couldn't say I was particularly displeased, but Renaud then said something else. "Look to your servant."

I turned to David and saw him clutching his throat as it was pouring blood.

Renaud had severed his throat.

Melissa, unable to control herself, launched herself at his neck and bit down on it.

"No!" I shouted, trying to stop her, but Renaud grabbed my arm and held me back.

"First he dies," Renaud whispered into my ear. "Then you do, Little Vampire."

CHAPTER SEVENTEEN

I could only watch helplessly as David had all of his blood drunk down by Melissa. I watched his arms flailing about before finally collapsing in rapturous joy as he became unable to resist the ecstasy of the Bite. I wanted to separate them—was willing to break my arm to do so, or rip it clean off—but something about Renaud's presence smothered me like a shroud. It was like his very presence drained away my strength and left me as weak and depressed as I had been in my mortal days.

Finally, after a seeming eternity, Melissa dropped David to the ground, and I felt our connection break. There was no life remaining in my friend. He just looked at me with cold, dead eyes. His face was a mixture of pleasure and terror, having died knowing he was being killed but still feeling immense pleasure the entire way through.

Jesus Christ.

I fell to my knees, my left arm still held by Renaud. Bloody tears welled in my eyes as I reached out with my other hand. "Why? Why, you sonofabitch? Why?"

Renaud finally let go.

"Because he was a servant to the race, which is accursed before God. Because he was a homosexual. Because he was a Jew on his mother's side. Because he was a product of this godless secular age. Take your pick of a hundred different reasons why your slave was worthy of death."

Melissa seemed to come out of the trance she'd been under when the Need had consumed her, perhaps aided by Renaud, perhaps not. She looked at her blood-covered hands, then down at the corpse of David before screaming.

Renaud let out a hearty laugh. "I applaud her misplaced sense of guilt and atonement. It is a sign I have chosen well for her to be one of the few to stay behind and torment mankind for its sins once we have been purified in the blood of the Nephilim."

I drew out my bone knife and launched myself at Renaud, stabbing him through his armor thanks to the enchantment on the knife. The knife sunk into his chest and into his heart. I started to twist it, only to have him grab both my hands.

"You know, that actually stings," Renaud said, delivering a vicious headbutt before looking into my eyes.

"Stay," Renaud said, his eyes possessing the power of hypnosis. I couldn't help but obey.

Melissa went for the grenade again, only to have Renaud stare at her. "Stop."

Melissa froze in place, crying tears of blood every bit as thick as mine.

"Persistent, aren't they?" the french-fry-eating clerk said, stealing David's wallet and going through the contents.

"Silence, Charles," Renaud said, his voice dismissive. "I want you to get all of the evidence from their car and burn it."

"You got it," Charles said. "I'll smash the laptop too."

Renaud proceeded to wrap both his hands around the bone dagger in his chest before slowly removing it. His face was contorted with agony as he did it, the first sign he was vulnerable at all, before he tossed the weapon to one side and the wound slowly healed up. There was no way he should be moving after being staked, but I'd been warned he didn't suffer any of the traditional vampiric weaknesses.

I just hadn't believed it.

"How?" I asked, trying desperately to move but paralyzed completely.

"A combination of factors," Renaud said, patting me on the head like a child. I hadn't imagined it possible for me to want to kill him more, but that act made me hate him more than I hated Eaton. Another thing I hadn't thought possible until the moment he did it. "Lamia's blood was stronger than the majority of our kind, so I awoke with the strength of an Old One. I was not truly immune to all of God's curses, though, until I met the First of the Gibborim under Jerusalem. The son of Lucifer and Lilith gave me a sword manufactured from his bone and gave me the power to drain the strength of other vampires as well as bestow that power unto those with whom I share my blood."

I actually managed a perverse chuckle. "Pal, I don't know what you've been smoking, but we've got this thing called the fossil record. There wasn't a Garden of Eden."

Renaud gave a dismissive wave. "The details of certain holy books may be inaccurate, but there are some literal truths that are worth believing in. Azazel, half-brother of Cain and Abel, gave me his tooth to drink of the flesh of vampires and restore his strength so that he might one day walk the Earth again to judge humanity for its sins."

"Dude, I met a vampire who was eight thousand years old once. He believed in Ra. Judeo-Christianity struck him as a fad."

Renaud's eyes narrowed. "To think I was going to offer you a chance to join my army of reborn and drink from the chalice of redemption."

"Your idea of redemption sucks."

Renaud gave a half-smile. "As you wish. Melissa, come to me."

Melissa struggled to resist Renaud but ended up marching robotically toward him. His blood ran through his veins from her creation, even if he hadn't stayed to finish the process, and his will was immensely powerful.

More powerful than mine.

"I hate you." Melissa spit blood in his face.

Renaud didn't react. "Love me."

Melissa looked like she was screaming inside. "No ... no."

Renaud's eyes blazed as he looked genuinely angry for the first time during this conversation. "Love me."

"Ah!" Melissa cried out.

"Love me!" Renaud repeated for a third time.

Like a puppet with its strings cut, Melissa dropped her arms and slumped over. "Yes. I love you."

"You fucking crypto-Nazi rapist!" I shouted, throwing myself at his control.

"I will not touch her," Renaud said, chuckling. "Not until she's had time to come terms with the price of her defiance. I have broken the wills of many women and men before and in time, they come to appreciate the power that comes with serving me. In time, they even come to love me of their own free will."

"Yeah, they call that Stockholm Syndrome now, you sick freak."

"Truth be told, I fully expected her to become a draugr and slaughter her way through the city," Renaud said, looking down at me. "It would have served as an excellent distraction for my plans. I didn't think a vampire would show compassion."

"So, why my place?" I really regretted missing this guy at the counter. I must have been stocking the freezer.

"My other mistress, Elisha, really hates you. She wanted my distraction to be in a place that would make you a figure of infamy until greater news overwhelmed you."

I was really starting to dislike my ex. "Yeah, well, sorry to disappoint your whole terrorist plan."

Renaud shrugged. "Fertilizer and other components of a bomb are hardly rare. Tomorrow or the next day is as good a time to do it as any. It's not like the Human Rights League's membership isn't replaceable. I'll do it in the morning this time, though."

I couldn't do anything but hate him in that moment and wish to God—yes, the God who burned me with every utterance of his name.

"Time to die," Renaud whispered, stretching out his hand. His sword flew to his hand. It was a twisted, curved scimitar-like weapon that vaguely resembled a giant vampire fang.

"You should frame him," Melissa said, her voice sad and empty.

Renaud swung his sword down onto my face, only to stop a few inches from my eyes. I couldn't even move to dodge, just let him bring down the weapon.

"Interesting," Renaud said, chuckling. "Frame him for what?"

"Killing Eaton," Melissa said, staring down at me. "Working with the Network. Covering up their crimes. Working with you to destroy the Council of Ancients. When they ask him what happened here tonight, you can leave a command in his mind for him to confess to being your catspaw."

"His master will see through that."

"Not if you have him implicate his master too."

Renaud chuckled. "Thoth is hosting the conference. Yes, that would make things most complicated for their defenses."

"You're never going to win," I said, shaking his head. "You can't wipe out dozens of Old Ones and Ancients. I don't care if you've got a magic tooth."

Renaud smiled. "This is where I could tell you why all of those vampires are going to be extraordinarily weak while my knights will be extraordinarily strong, isn't it?"

"Yeah, if you don't mind."

"I do," Renaud said. "Sorry."

That was when I saw in Melissa's mind as she saw in Renaud's mind. She was trying to read him and then project into my mind.

I saw a desecrated Baptist church with numerous bodies hanging upside down on hooks, their throats slit and draining blood down into a series of baptismal fonts and garden fountains that had been spread about the place. The place was covered in spray-painted hermetic diagrams and crude Kabbalistic perversions.

Through Melissa's eyes, I recognized all of the people being sacrificed as the family members of the Humanity First Members who had gone on to conduct the terrorist attack against the Apophis. Renaud had used his influence with the congregation to summon them all for slaughter like animals, using the massacre to fuel some kind of spell.

Shit.

Renaud wore a Catholic Cardinal's robes, blood stains almost invisible against its crimson, as he stood before a congregation of the Network's members I'd seen in The Razor. They were all standing in line, lifting up plastic wine glasses of the blood drained around them before holding the glasses to their mouths.

Elisha was among them.

Goddammit, Lisha.

Renaud addressed the crowd before him. "You have heard 'blood of my blood, flesh of my flesh.' This is true. I have dropped a thimble full of my blood into each of these fonts and worked the rights to invoke the power of the One Who Sleeps.

"There are those of you who do not believe in the Nephilim, believe him to be one of the Elder Gods which came to this dimension long ago and became trapped, but I say thee nay. Know the power I give you is divine. It will render you immune to all of the weaknesses of vampires as well as allow me to bestow upon you a portion of my strength without diminishing mine."

"Will it be enough?" one rather stupid biker asked in the back of the crowd.

Renaud smiled, though I could tell he was furious about being interrupted. "The power from this sacrifice will make you every bit as powerful as the Old Ones. The Ancient Ones will also be crippled, I can assure you."

In Renaud's mind, I knew he fully expected the Network soldiers here to die. They would be as strong as he said, but they were cannon fodder while he drank the power of the Ancient Ones and slaughtered them. He only needed them distracted long enough to kill a few of the oldest of the vampire race and he would be unstoppable. The worst-case scenario would be having to flee and leaving them to their fate. He would regret leaving Elisha behind, but she was a whore, unlike Melissa, and unworthy of anything but the basest attention.

God damn, this guy was an asshole.

Melissa and I both tried to probe deeper into his mind to find out what he was doing to the Ancients to make them docile. Instead, I got images of him screaming out as he was tortured in prison and subjected to every form of nightmarish abuse imaginable. From hot pokers to rape to daily beatings, they tried to get him to confess to demon worship in order to frame the Templars for diabolism.

Vampires were among the torturers.

I saw Lamia, only the indistinct outline of her, but easily the most beautiful woman in the world, bite into his neck. Not for release, but because she found his persistent faith in God amusing. I saw his wife deny him at his trial for witchcraft before he was burned alive, regenerating to feast on a host of innocents thereafter. Totally insane for years thereafter. Sleeping in barns, killing those he encountered, and living like an animal until his mind returned.

Somewhat.

I saw Renaud struggle to live off vampire blood and protect the innocent, only to be rewarded time and time again with betrayal as well as horror from those he wanted to protect. I saw him end up feeding on the innocent over and over again because he could not control his hunger when denying himself the blood of humans.

I saw him seek a cure for vampirism in Jerusalem.

I saw the outline of a thing that was so terrifying that the creature inside my body, the monster that animated my form, leapt out of our connection.

Shit, that was fucked up.

Renaud's eyes flashed and he grabbed me by the throat with his free hand. "Have you been in my mind, newborn?"

I coughed. "Uh, no. I didn't see you riding the misery train."

Okay, why did I say that? That wasn't going to help me.

Renaud looked at Melissa before shaking his head and holding his sword to one side. "What did you think of what you saw?"

"I think you got a raw deal. However, I also know plenty of other people who suffered almost as bad. Gina the mage was in a goddamn camp in Serbia, for example. He didn't turn into a fucking psychopath. So … what's wrong with you?"

Renaud sliced across my chest with his sword and it felt like someone was pouring napalm into the cut.

I screamed.

Renaud dropped me. "The Tooth of Azazel will not kill you, but it will make you wish for death. You will call to your creator with your blood, and then when you are interrogated by the City Council, you will condemn him before it as well as confess your crimes. You will even believe this yourself when they ask you. Do you understand?"

"Yes," I said. "Absolutely."

Worse, I meant it.

Thoth had never used our bond to influence my will, preferring words, and even voivode Ashura had avoided using anything but subtle glamours against me. This was the first time I had someone reach into my mind and then TWIST it into obedience. It was a nightmare I wouldn't wish on anyone.

Let alone myself.

"Come, Melissa," Renaud said, holding out his sword as it levitated back into the sheath on his back.

Which defeated the purpose of a sheath, in my opinion. If the damned thing required magic to use, then why have it?

Melissa reluctantly complied. "I would like to say it was a pleasure meeting with you, Peter, but I would be lying. This was a most unpleasant experience all around."

"Ditto, babe."

Renaud then took her by the arm and leapt into the air.

The two of them went flying off.

"Oh hell no!" I shouted up in the air. "You do not get actual flight too! I do not care how old you are or how many demons you've screwed!"

But he was gone.

The wound on my chest festered, and I couldn't help but look over to the dead body of my best friend. It was a living nightmare and I wanted it to end. David was dead because I'd brought him into this demented, horrifying world. This was the second time in my life I truly regretted accepting Thoth's offer. If I hadn't, I'd probably had gone down in a hail of violence trying to avenge my brother, but David would be alive. Hell, it might have even impacted this bullshit wannabe parody of every vampire-hunting-vampire-ever-made's plans.

Self-hating vampires were the worst.

"I'm sorry, David," I whispered, closing my eyes. "Forgive me."

He didn't respond, of course, because he was dead.

Jumping Jack Flash then spoke, the last voice I expected to hear. "Yep, right where I saw him. I hate being right."

"Shut up and help me get him into the truck," Kali's voice spoke next.

"As you wish. This isn't going to keep the Network from being destroyed, you realize."

"Right now, I'm just trying to prove we're better than what Renaud is trying to make us."

I would have smiled, but I knew Kali was going to take me right to Thoth, which played into Renaud's hands.

"What about the servant?" Jumping Jack Flash asked, surprisingly coherent.

"Him too. I have some questions to ask his ghost."

His what?

CHAPTER EIGHTEEN

Vampires don't dream. When the sun rises, we feel an urge to find some place cold and dark before we die. That's the only way to describe it. A vampire in the daytime is as dead as a guy in a coffin—no pun intended—although it is possible for a few things to awaken them out of sheer survival instinct. We don't return to life—unlife—until the sun sets. With my blood curdling from the wound I'd received, I was as good as dead.

But I dreamed.

It was yet another one of my insipid flashbacks. I was starting to wonder if they were related to my time-manipulation powers, powers that had conspicuously failed to do jack and shit against Renaud. It was a meeting with Thoth back when I was still a newborn vampire trying to find my way in the world. The two of us were meeting in a back booth of the Apophis's largest restaurant.

Both of us had ordered coffee with an extra mug. The whole "swish and spit" thing was kind of disgusting, but I had to admit the flavors a vampire tongue could pick up on were amazing. I'd once accidentally swallowed, though, and spent an hour dry-heaving. It was enough that I rarely bothered to try and taste what I'd left behind.

"I want you to infiltrate the Network," Thoth said, his voice casual. "I didn't think that would be a hard concept to understand."

I shook my head. "I'm just wondering why the hell I would do a thing like that."

It had been three months since the last of the Network Riots, and the war had settled down. The Network had completely surrendered New Detroit, Milwaukee, Chicago, and a bunch of other cities to the Vampire Nation. The terms negotiated would provide large amounts of supernatural labor for the building of New Detroit as well as long-term labor contracts for future projects. There were other concessions too, things involving contracts written in blood as well as robed torchlight ceremonies. I *hated* robed torchlight ceremonies.

"Please tell me you're not still upset about your financial situation," Thoth said, dismissing me with about the same level of disdain as John Hammond had for Dennis Nedry in *Jurassic Park*. God, I had to stop watching sci-fi movies with my new roommate. David was a cool guy, but he had to realize there were other things than TV in this world. Speaking of which, was that Terrance Howard? Awesome. I needed to go over there and say hello.

I needed to give Thoth the business first, though. "You mean the fact you make me immortal and then fire me? As well as tell no other businesses in Detroit to hire me?"

"I said not to hire you in businesses I run," Thoth said. "Not to not hire you at all."

"You run half of New Detroit and the other half is scared of you."

"You flatter me."

"Why did you fire me, T?" I asked, genuinely confused. "It's been a pretty hellish three months going from Armani suits to blue jeans and t-shirts again."

The worst—or best—part of it was the Network had been there for me. Even though it had lost the majority of its funding, hundreds of members, and had been through the ringer financially. It had carried on its mission to help the supernaturals of Detroit.

That had included me.

I'd also met a hot young firebrand named Elisha.

I thought we'd had something.

Thoth looked introspective. "To be honest, I think of it as a sort of test. It's all too easy to come to take for granted the perks of immortality and assume they are rights rather than privileges. Unlike most vampires, I had to build myself up from nothing. I want to give you the opportunity to do the same."

Great. He'd done it because he'd wanted to teach me a lesson about appreciating what I had. Goddammit. "Then allow me to give you the opportunity of being told to piss off. Oh right, we don't do that anymore. The Network has my back."

Thoth smiled, which showed he was different from just about every other Old One. "Fond of your Network associates now, are you?"

"Yeah, well, they don't know that. You guys did a real number on them."

"That was the plan, yes. They wanted to carve an equal society here in New Detroit where every supernatural had his or her own say in the way our businesses and government are run."

"Yeah, those monsters," I said, shaking my head. "How awful of them."

"Yes," Thoth said. "Because we are not a nation of equals. Every Old One has proven the ability to survive immense changes in history, society, and culture. They have also survived a society built on dog-eat-dog principles. The fact that they had a fortune that appeared large enough to bail out the United States—"

"What do you mean 'appeared'?"

Thoth ignored that comment. "—is all part of their display. I have seen the tyranny of the majority every bit as well as the tyranny of the few and prefer the latter."

"Only because you're one of the few."

"Indeed." Thoth didn't deny it. "But if a man is going to destroy my life, I want it to be because he personally hates me and not because he wants to sign a bill into law that says all vampires must be staked or all of my assets should be shared with the poor."

"Even it was made on the backs of the poor," I said.

"It is easy to rob the poor," Thoth said. "Less so to work with them, as I have tried to do. It is easy to see the underdog as the hero, but a man who is eaten by starving wolves is no less the victim, especially when they could hunt for food together."

"I'm leaving. I don't have time for this Obi-Wan crap."

"The Network is a branch of the Vampire Nation. I fund ninety-percent of its activities in Michigan."

I stared at him. "You son of a bitch."

"The Network Riots were necessary."

"You got hundreds of people killed," I said, staring at him. "You're dead to me."

"I am already dead," Thoth said. "I did not incite the riots, merely took advantage of the fact every dollar they spent came from me as well as the fact that the organization was littered with spies. The Bailout resulted in an unprecedented amount of pressure on the Vampire Nation to bring to heel those who had come out of the coffin."

"Don't quote *True Blood* at me."

"The simple fact was that we needed everyone on the same page for a singular set of laws to apply to us all. The Network was created to direct the voices of the supernatural masses so they could campaign for issues the Old Ones agreed with."

"They're your Tea Party. There to get the voters all enthused before you vote on the same old shit you want while letting them think you changed everything."

"Essentially, yes."

"Then how did we get to the Riots?"

"I was overruled," Thoth said, frowning. "The Council of Ancients wanted a war to justify killing as many poor and weak-blooded supernaturals as possible."

"Fuck those assholes."

"It was to prevent the United States from ordering a general purge of us all."

My eyes widened. "What?"

"We have spent one hundred and twenty years playing the long game," Thoth said, frowning. "Ever since Vlad came up with the idea of using his vanity project to make vampires look heroic. Revelation was inevitable from the time the first photographs and voice recordings appeared, so we wanted it to happen on our terms. Even so, when we finally revealed ourselves, the United States government barely voted down a secret measure to test all citizens for supernatural blood, then execute the positives. Regardless of whether they were dangerous forms of supernaturals or not. From psychics to demonkind."

"You serious?"

"As death, Peter, yes. As so many minorities have learned over the course of history, money is not power. It can certainly make your life easier, but it cannot protect you from the truly committed bigot."

"This still doesn't explain the Network slaughter."

"We do not have our own court system and legal code because we want to protect the Vampire Nation's power base," Thoth said, before correcting himself. "Not entirely, at least. It's to keep the United States from being able to judge us. They are not our peers, let alone a jury of them. To achieve that sort of separate—"

"But equal status?"

"Ha ha," Thoth said, not at all amused. "We had to make compromises. That included regulating our kind with a firm hand."

"That was mass murder, not regulation."

Thoth sighed. "Yes, it was. It was a war the Network couldn't hope to win, but still drew out all of the fools who thought the government was their friend rather their enemy. Things are silent for now, especially with the Network, and will allow us to solidify our position. That includes keeping our numbers low, numbers that exploded when everyone and their uncle was begging their newly revealed vampire friends to be changed."

"Sounds like we're doing the government's work for it."

"We are," Thoth said, baring one of his fangs in distaste. "Don't think for a second I don't loathe each and every one of the actions undertaken. I also think the Council of Ancients betrayed their people by letting the weakest of our kind be fed to the wolves to save their own skins. To make us look like we were their lackeys, which was exactly what we were. I've arranged for the ruination and death of only a quarter of the government officials who voted for the extermination of our kind, but I'm confident I'll eventually get to them all. Patience is the key."

My eyes widened as I remembered the plane crash that had killed a half-dozen senators along with their staffs, plus the unusually high number of sex scandals that had resulted in the torching of wholesale sections of the Democratic as well as Republican parties.

"Damn," I said.

"Take your revenge cold," Thoth said. "It is finer that way."

"You a Klingon, T?"

Thoth looked at me confused.

"Never mind," I said. "So you want me to help you lead the Network to slaughter? Screw that."

"The Network has already been slaughtered," Thoth said, looking ill. "The Remnant is what concerns us now. There are still many in the City Council alone who would like to see them eradicated to the last and intend to play them off against other gangs."

"Who?" I said, growling.

A light seemed to dawn past Thoth's eyes. "Ah, this is about a woman ... or man."

"Woman," I said. "Not that there's anything wrong with the other. I mean, if you're into that. Which I'm not."

"If you say so." Thoth gave a dismissive shrug of his shoulders. "I have my preferences as well, albeit everything goes during the Danse Macabre."

Ah, yes. The yearly vampire social.

Thoth continued. "I do believe we have some responsibility to the Young Bloods and lesser supernatural races."

"Lesser races?"

"It's not biased if it's accurate," Thoth said. "I want you to steer them away from conflict if you can and report on them to me. The others will try and manipulate them into war, and I'd like to see them survive until the New Dusk."

I frowned. "It sounds like you're trying to convince me I'm doing them a favor by spying on them."

"You are," Thoth said. "But you'll also be paid for it."

I was silent. I hated myself for what I asked after about a minute. "How much?"

The number was right.

"So much for earning my way on my own," I muttered.

"This will be earning it," Thoth said, coolly. "It requires a special kind of resolve to lie, cheat, and steal from those you care for while still caring for them. It's not a kind of attitude I enjoyed cultivating, but it's helped me survive."

"At what cost?"

"Too high at times," Thoth replied. "Are you in or are you out?"

"In," I muttered, drinking my coffee then spitting it right back out into the mug. "Damn you."

"Good."

"Why do you care so much about all this either way?" I asked. "The government, the Network, all of it."

"That is a story for another time," Thoth said. "But as much as I hate humans, I also love them. We are the product of their clay. I have suffered unimaginable indignities at their hands and known great loves. I have no cause to love the United States government, let alone the other countries of the world where vampirism is outright banned, but we will need them as well as the Young Bloods in the decades ahead."

"Something else happening?"

"Perhaps," Thoth said, a distant look in his eyes. "There have been stirrings in the astral plane and underground. The modern vampire race is only eight thousand years old, starting with Lamia. There are older things than us, though. Ancient horrors that built cities as farms and created genetic bottlenecks with the endlessness of their hungers. If kept propagated, they remain quiescent, but I fear they will not remain so indefinitely. We must be prepared for them."

"Wow, that got dark."

"The Elder Gods are a dark topic," Thoth replied. "At least state-sponsored mass murder is something I have familiarity with. Humanity never seems to get over that one."

Elisha arrived moments later, wearing a stunning red dress and pumps, a sharp contrast to her usual attire—something she was wearing to impress me. She sat down beside me and did her best to keep her disgust at Thoth's presence from showing on her face.

"Hello," Elisha said. "So, you're Peter's jerk-ass creator."

"In the flesh," Thoth said, not at all perturbed by her.

"What were you two discussing?" Elisha asked.

"How the Vampire Nation is secretly keeping Cthulhu under wraps," I said, already feeling like a traitor.

Elisha kissed me, I kissed back.

Thoth got up from the table. "I was never a fan of H. P. Lovecraft's writings. Enormous racist. I do have a small fondness for Robert E. Howard, though. If you'll excuse me, I have business to attend to."

I told Elisha a story about how Thoth was trying to get me to leave her association because it wasn't good for me to be seen hanging with the Network. I also told her I'd told him to take a flying leap into the sun. The lying came easy to me and would continue to do so for the next year or so of our relationship.

I deserved everything Elisha wanted to do to me, but her plan with Renaud, whatever it was, wasn't going to work. They might slaughter all of the city's Old Ones and maybe a couple of Ancient Ones visiting from Romania, but they wouldn't be able to get them all. It would result in the destruction of all the Network in retaliation—probably their families too.

I had to stop it.

That was when I woke up in a room filled with sunlight.

CHAPTER NINETEEN

I woke up on the ground in the middle of a room filled with daylight. For a brief second I thought I was going to die, until I realized all of the daylight was streaming down from UV lamps enhanced with magic and formed a perfect square in the center of the room. None of it was directly touching me, but it was still enough to freak me the hell out. I mean, imagine being surrounded in every direction by fire. That's how sunlight felt to a vampire.

I recognized the Cage of Ra, which is what this particular device was called. It was a device for keeping vampires subdued until they could be transported for judgment on their various crimes. Given there were only a few laws in the Vampire Nation and almost all of them carried the death penalty, this was less a holding cell and more death row.

I remembered all of the events with Renaud in rapid succession, recalling the horror of watching David killed before my eyes and being helpless to do anything about it. Worse, I knew when they interrogated me I would say I was helping Renaud the entire time. I'd say Thoth was involved and probably implicate a bunch of other people I liked.

That was the nature of my command. It was in my head, buried there, an impossible-to-ignore directive like *Robocop* being unable to arrest a senior employee of OCP. Which doesn't count as a sci-fi movie but as a Detroit movie.

God, I was going to miss David.

I ran my fingers over my chest and found someone had carved the corrupted flesh off my chest. I still felt weak from the Tooth of Azazel's (God, that was a stupid name) touch, but I wasn't starving for blood either. I noted a couple of holes in my arm and I guessed they had given me a few IVs to make sure I recovered.

So they could kill me themselves.

Standing up, I took a deep breath to power my shout. "Hey! I'm awake in here! I need to talk to someone!"

Nothing happened.

Great.

I turned out to be impatient, though, because a door opened in the wall and Jumping Jack Flash walked in. He was wearing a long white trench coat, his fedora with a little red feather, and a white puffy shirt with black leather pants. He had a pair of sunglasses on to protect him from the sunlight he was standing in.

Not a vampire then. Bloodsworn? Shapechanger? What was he?

"Great, another round of absolute insane drivel from the bar fly pimp," I muttered looking down.

"Well if you don't want to talk, Stone, I can just leave you to your fate," Jumping Jack Flash said, perfectly coherent.

"So, the crazy prophet thing is an act."

Jumping Jack Flash shrugged. "Not really. I can see the future, but it's safer to be thought a drunk fool than a man who can genuinely predict what will happen."

I stared at him. "Do you know how tonight will end?"

"In fire," Jumping Jack Flash said.

Babylon Five fan?" I asked.

Jumping Jack Flash chuckled. "That's one of the things you'll hate about growing old. You'll develop a massive number of pop culture references no one else will get."

"How's that?"

"I do a mean Buster Keaton impression. Used to be hilarious."

"Ah."

"So, where am I and what am I in for?" I asked, dreading the answer.

I tried not to think about David or Melissa. Even though I'd known the latter for a single night, it was horrifying to imagine what was her potential next few centuries as Renaud's prisoner. I'd royally fucked up my priorities tonight, and Eaton's death barely registered as an accomplishment.

"Kali and I brought you to the voivode, who scanned your mind. She found out you were involved in the bombing attempt on the Apophis, you killed Eaton, and that you were working with the Network to kill everyone involved in the Walpurgis Night meeting."

"Shit," I said, grimacing. "I—"

"Of course, they know you're not guilty."

"Wait, what?"

"Kali contacted the ghost of your slave," Jumping Jack Flash said.

"Servant," I corrected. "David left a ghost?"

"Everyone does," Jumping Jack Flash said. "Heaven and Hell are really just names for how screwed you are post-death as well as where the spirits take you."

"That's ... terrifying."

"You should ask your creator about his journey to hell sometime," Jumping Jack Flash said. "Anyway, he revealed everything which happened with Renaud and that you were brainwashed into incriminating yourself."

"Oh, that's good," I said, staring.

"Yes, too bad it didn't help your situation."

I blinked. "Explain that one, please?"

"Indian necromancy is not permissible for use in Vampire Nation courts. Also, the testimony of Rakshasa is considered inadmissible."

"Are you kidding me?"

"I didn't make the rules. Rakshasas are one of the few races in the world as numerous, powerful, and rich as vampires. It doesn't help that India's probably going to be the new superpower of the twenty-second century while the undead are stuck with the USA. Either way, they've sentenced you to die anyway."

I grit my teeth. "What about Renaud?"

"Oh, they're going to take precautions against him and move the meeting," Jumping Jack Flash said. "I mean, they're not stupid."

I closed my eyes and let out a gallows laugh. "This is because of Eaton, isn't it? I was involved in his death and the voivode blames me for killing her child."

"Yeah, probably. I've known Ashura for a long time and she's not someone who gives up on her romances easily."

"She should have chosen better."

"You didn't know Eaton during the Nineteenth Century. He was a dashing cavalryman and Southern aristocrat. She was all into the

Gone with the Wind thing with him. Right up until it fell out of favor and she abandoned him for the next flavor of the month. You know she has a perfect reproduction of Tara down in Georgia?"

"That doesn't surprise me in the slightest," I said, disgusted. "Is there any chance of me getting out of this?"

"Not that I see," Jumping Jack Flash said. "Then again, it's a matter less of genuine love than of pride, which is worse. There probably is a solution, but you're not rich, powerful, or well-connected enough to afford it."

"Wow, that actually makes it worse."

"Sorry," Jumping Jack Flash said, removing a flask from his coat. "I'd offer you some, but I don't want you spitting on the floor."

I shook my head, too tired to really care at this point. Either that or the sunlight around me was sapping my strength. "Well, since I'm probably going to be staked, decapitated, burned alive, and left out for the sun—"

"Don't forget your mouth filled with communion wafers and verbena."

I blanched. "Okay, that's just overkill."

"Agreed."

"Will you answer me a question that's been bugging me?" I didn't have much else to do in here, so I might as well make chit-chat. It was better than the alternative of ruminating over David's death and Melissa's abduction. It was amazing how jaded you got about unlife when you were a vampire.

"Yes, I would have gone out with you if you'd asked. I'm afraid you would have found the evening terribly dull, though, toward the end." Jumping Jack Flash gave me a handsome smile of his all-too-perfect teeth, which I imagined David would have found immensely appealing.

Dammit.

When was the jadedness going to kick in?

I wanted it now.

"What? Wait, no! Actually, I wanted to know what the hell you were."

"If you want to die denying how you feel, certainly." Jumping Jack Flash chuckled. "I am one of the Accursed."

"One of the what now?" I had met a lot of weird things in the years I'd been a vampire, but this was a new one. One of these days I was really going to have go on the Internet and spend a few nights figuring out just what the hell was real and not.

Leprechauns were real, for example.

But assholes. Every last one of them.

Jumping Jack Flash got a wistful look in his eye. "I am human, for the most part, but when I was a young aristocrat in rural France, I was less than kind to my fellow man. After one night of drunkenness with my fellows, I was cursed by a witch who was the mother of a young girl I'd defiled. She told me I would never be able to love or give love ever again. Furthermore, that I would live forever until I committed suicide."

"My heart bleeds for you," I said, sarcastically. "I never quite understood curses that include an immortality clause. It didn't make sense in *The Mummy* with Brendan Fraser and it doesn't make sense here."

"Yes, well, psychopathia was poorly understood in the seventeenth century, so it worked out well for me." Jumping Jack Flash shrugged. "I admit, it did come with the downside of permanent impotence, but life is a great deal more than sex, so I suppose you could say I learned my lesson."

"Right," I said, wondering why the hell I was behind bars and he was free. Oh right, because the world wasn't right or fair. "How did you end up working for the vampires?"

"Once it was discovered that my blood had no enticement for the undead or nourishment value, apparently qualifying as a form of love, they realized I was the perfect sort of infiltrator and emissary for their daylight activities."

"A spy, you mean."

"Very much so," Jumping Jack Flash said. "I was living the life of Dorian Gray in Queen Vic's London, minus the sex part of course, when they found me. I wasn't really interested in it because my work in the slave trade centuries prior had set me up for—"

I really wanted to break his neck right then. "Uh huh."

Jumping Jack Flash noticed my anger. He covered his heart and looked apologetic. "Not that I had anything against African peoples, mind you! I would have enslaved anyone to make money."

I let my mouth hang open, unsure if that made it better or worse.

Jumping Jack Flash sighed. "In the end, they made the proverbial offer I couldn't refuse. It turns out that whole suicide clause looks awfully attractive when they promise to cut off your head and then bury it in the concrete of a bridge for all eternity. I've been gainfully employed as their servant ever since."

"I am genuinely sorry I asked."

"If you want, I could prophesize your doom."

"I'd prefer you to prophesize my getting the fuck out of here."

"Doom isn't always negative in its original meaning," Jumping Jack Flash said, once more pulling out his deck of cards and shuffling them. "I've picked up a lot of tricks living with my curse as long as I have, and true sight is one of them. Of course, knowing what happens to true prophets, I do my best to make my visions as inaccurate as I can without completely destroying my credibility."

My mouth was dry and I was tempted, truly tempted, to ask him what was going to happen to me. "No. No, I'll find out for myself."

Jumping Jack Flash's smile actually became wistful. "Perhaps a good thing. I, out of boredom, once prophesized my own fate and got my answer."

"Which was?"

"Eventually, I will commit suicide. That—knowing that I will someday become so bored or depressed life will have no meaning—has turned more wine and food to ash in my mouth than any witch's curse."

"World's smallest violin, Rapey-Boy."

"If you don't want company, that's your prerogative." Jack put away his flask and turned to leave.

"Why did you help me, anyway?" I asked. "You informed on us at The Razor. We could have slipped out of there without your warning."

Jack gave a half-smile as he reached the door. "The true answer? It seemed like something to do at the time. I think Elisha is doing the right thing trying to slaughter the Ancients, even if she's going to fail. I also think Kali is doing the right thing by trying to make peace with the various supernatural factions in the city. The real trick to mastering immortality is learning that since everyone is doing what they think is right, the best thing you can do is anything you want."

"That's a horrible life philosophy."

"It works for me."

Jack was about to depart when all of the sunlight lamps in the chamber turned off and the door opened, causing him to take a step back. That was when Thoth entered, wearing a white suit and looking like someone had told him the mortgage was due and he wasn't a billionaire vampire casino owner.

Jack tipped his hat before departing.

"I think he's stealing your outfits," I said, pointing at the Accursed. "You should totally bury him alive for that."

Thoth gave a half-smile. "You're free to go."

I stared at him. "OK, you really need to work on your messenger system, since Jumping Jack Flash just told me I was going to be executed for a bunch of shit I didn't do because vampires are racist dickbags."

"That was the case," Thoth said, walking over to me and putting his hand on his shoulder. "But I resolved it. I'm sorry about David. He was a good servant."

"No, he wasn't," I said.

"No, he wasn't," Thoth agreed. "But he might have made a good vampire."

"That he would have," I admitted. "Now he's in Heaven."

"Well, probably not."

"That's a shit thing to say."

"It's not a statement meant to depress you. Just a statement of fact. All vampires and their servants go to hell," Thoth said, definitely.

"I take it you're speaking literally? Jack mentioned you once visited Hell."

"Yes, I once died during a battle with the Nazis in Russia—"

"And you say it so casually."

Thoth shrugged. "My first wife, Lucinda, journeyed to the Underworld to lead me out. I got a Dante-esque view of what it was like."

"Uh huh." I wondered where this was going.

"The entirety of Hell is a shopping center."

I blinked. "What?"

Thoth said, "It takes various forms, mind you, but from Babylon onward, marketplaces have always been the worst place in the universe for the mundane petty annoyances of life. Millions of mindless consumers shambled through this one, while stores were run by souls of exceptional quality. It was my eternal punishment to be the snooty jewelry store owner who always gets asked to show customers things they obviously can't afford."

I stared at him. "Now you're pulling my leg. Also, I hate that guy."

"He hates you too," Thoth said. "I regret to say that a succubus whispered to me your punishment, Peter, even though you hadn't been born yet. She said you would be forced to forever guard the souls of the damned."

"My eternal punishment is to be a mall cop."

"So it seems."

"That sounds better than my current life."

Thoth shrugged. "Either way, I'm a believer in Voudan, so I have an out when and if I ever die again."

"You're going to have to qualify that story sometime. Like how the hell, no pun intended, you got back. Is there, uh, anything we can do for David?"

Thoth was silent.

"That's what I thought," I said, frowning. "Hopefully, he's a manager down there at least. So, how did you get me out of here?"

"I gave away half my fortune."

Sometimes there were no words.

CHAPTER TWENTY

My eyes widened. "You gave up half your fortune for me?" That wasn't just a chunk of change; that was Scrooge McDuck money bin levels of cash. Thoth not only owned the Apophis but also had been there in Silicon Valley at the start, where he floated money toward Gates as well as Jobs (both of whom were of the undead persuasion now) in exchange for a part of their empires. He'd also been there to negotiate everything from diamonds to oil to Nixon opening up China on behalf of the Vampire Nation.

Damn.

Thoth gave a dismissive gesture. "It's not that big of a deal."

"The hell it's not," I said, shaking my head. "Who did you give it to?"

"Voivode Ashura," Thoth said, as if the answer wasn't obvious. "She was the one demanding your head and the one who controls who lives and who dies in the city. I made a proposal of marriage to her, casually mentioning how awful it would be to execute her son by such a union."

I was suddenly less sympathetic. "Marriage isn't giving away half your fortune, T."

"Clearly, you haven't experienced it as it is done among vampires or just about any culture prior to the modern era and even then some. Vampires are old-fashioned. There is one dominate partner in marriage and one submissive. For the next hundred years, she'll have access to my funds and the ability to request whatever she wants from me in service. At the end of a century, when our marriage dissolves, she will claim three-quarters of our assets."

OK, that actually sounded worse than just giving her half of his fortune. "I'm sorry, T."

Thoth looked away, clearly uncomfortable with this line of conversation. "Like I said, it's not that big of a deal. I've had far worse masters than Ashura, and she's pleasant enough company. She only wants access to my fortune to prop up hers as well as the occasional bit of companionship. Vampires, thankfully, aren't hung up on notions of monogamy. I won't have to divorce my other brides."

"Your what now?"

"You already know Fatimah. She really shouldn't count, as it was the product of a boozy night of feeding in Jamaica, but it's still legal on paper. That reminds me—I should send her harem a present. One of her brides is pregnant and a dhampyr is always a cause for celebration."

I was ninety percent sure he was screwing with me. "How does that work?"

"Well, obviously any child born of a blood servant is going to have a vampire's blood running through their veins anyway, but Fatimah also likes shapeshifting so—"

"I withdraw all questions."

Thoth smiled. "You should find yourself a vampire bride. Not too early, though. I don't think anyone is really ready to take one until they're at least a century old."

"Could we focus on murdering the hell out of Renaud and getting Melissa back?"

"You really want to help her?"

I was surprised by that statement, but I suppose she was just another vampire hunter to Thoth.

"She tried to help me even when Renaud was completely dominating me," I said, trying to explain why it was important. "I learned all about a magic tooth sword, Renaud—"

"Yeah, we saw all of that," Thoth said. "It's very helpful information, even though it basically just amounts to Renaud being even more of an unstoppable killing machine than he was before."

"I swear, he's like a video game character come to life. If he had white hair and made quips, we'd be truly fucked."

"*Devil May Cry's* Dante is a half-demon, not a vampire."

I paused. "OK, seriously, how the hell do you know that?"

"What? A two-hundred-year old vampire can't own a gaming console?"

"No!" I said, appalled at the way my mentor was ruining my fantasy of him. "You have orgies and shit to attend to!"

Thoth shrugged. "You have to learn about time management in these sorts of things. You have to do something to fill your daytimes as an Old One when the rest of your kind has fallen asleep. I just like watching supernatural programs and these little fantasy games people are building with computers now. Life can't all be sex, drugs, blood, and parties."

"I'm pretty sure it can, actually."

"It gets old."

"It does not!"

Thoth laughed and walked to the door. "In any case, we've doubled security, moved the location of the Walpurgis meeting, added extra wards to the walls, and also arranged for some military hardware to be brought over to arm our soldiers. Our current location is several hundred feet under the New Detroit Airport in a private bunker built for the President of the United States, so it's very likely Renaud won't be able to find us before the Ancients leave."

That didn't actually reassure me. "Renaud isn't going to be content to cancel his plan. He as good as told me he's going to try to blow up the Apophis again."

Thoth looked dejected. "If we were to try to round up a group of people capable of killing Renaud, then now would probably be the best time to try. I won't lie to you—the Council of Ancients has always been interested in letting him do his business as long as he's killing Young Bloods. Even when he kills Old Ones, the Ancients consider it eliminating competition."

"Which is why Renaud is going to start attacking Ancient Ones. He's sick of not doing enough damage to make a difference."

"Convincing them of that is the hard part."

"I can track him," I said, staring at Thoth. "I can reach out to Melissa and she's connected to him. We can find this son of a bitch and end him."

Thoth stared at me, still standing in front of the door. "All right. I'll help you."

"What?"

"Renaud came within inches of destroying everything we have.

Not just you and me but vampiredom in general. Even if he terrifies me—and he does—I can't let him get away. Not when he'll just come back stronger and stronger thanks to that Elder God weapon he's got."

"You'll have to explain the whole Elder God thing some day."

"They're a bunch of really old gods."

I rolled my eyes. "Not helpful."

"They're bad. Don't wake them up or feed them or they'll eat the planet."

"We're living in *Buffy*?"

"Closer than you'd think. Renaud is one of their puppets, like Lamia was in the old days before the Ancients overthrew her rule. They were the beings we worshiped before we realized the only people we should worship was ourselves or the small gods of humanity."

"Remember what I said earlier about withdrawing all questions? Yeah, I repeat that."

"Understood." Thoth finally opened the door and walked out while I followed. The hallway beyond was long and dark with minimal lighting, the way vampires preferred it. The air was cool too, like a cellar, and devoid of toxins. Vampires didn't breathe, absorbing all the oxygen they needed from blood, but preferred their air as clean as possible for some reason. "We'll need allies for this, Peter. Also magic, something to drain away his power or otherwise weaken him. Which is difficult since he doesn't have any vampire weaknesses."

I knew approximately jack and shit about magic and jack had left town. "Your knife caused him pain when I stuck it into his heart. Not enough to incapacitate him, but it sure as hell hurt him."

"That's oddly reassuring." Thoth then produced the kukri I'd left behind on the ground at Burgertown and handed it over.

I took it. "It's about as useful as a slingshot, but I'll take it."

"Even those can defeat Goliath. We just need to figure a way to amp up its power."

"Or just find out where he is and convince the government to drop a few hellfire missiles on his head."

"That might slow him down, at least. Yes. Come, let us go speak to some Ancients."

The hallway opened up to a massive underground chamber that contained literal fountains of blood, buffets of hypnotized humans standing perfectly still in rows, and nude statues made of purest silver. The statues were enchanted to even my untrained senses, as everything became sharper and more potent around them. Somehow, they seemed to strengthen the very idea of vampirism.

There were a hundred undead from all across the Vampire Nation in elaborate period clothes custom-tailored for tonight. It was like all those movies where they were frozen in their fashion sense from life, but here it was vibrant and alive (in a manner of speaking), like the Vampire Halloween. There were vampires from the Middle East, Africa, the Caribbean, Eastern Europe, and China. Strangely—and I couldn't make this up if I tried—the 70s Alicia Bridges disco tune "I Love the Nightlife" was playing.

"Is that real blood?" I asked, staring at the fountains. "Won't that cause a riot?"

"Artificial blood," Thoth answered, surveying the party. "It doesn't have the same effect on vampires and is even less nourishing than animal blood. Everyone can sense it. It does, however, make an excellent party favor."

"Huh," I said. "Learn something new every day."

"It's not exactly the most interesting party I've ever attended, but the Vampire Nation is a pyramid scheme and you have to suck up—no pun intended—to those above you if you're to get anything done."

"Is Dracula here?" I asked, figuring there was a decent shot.

"That preening prima donna? Hell no," Thoth said, wrinkling his nose. "He's too busy smiling for the cameras and delivering whatever ridiculous speech he thinks is doing the cause good from Romania's Supernatural Autonomous Zone."

"How's that working out for him?"

"Turkey keeps trying to extradite him for war crimes."

"Damn, you'd think there'd be a statute of limitations for that."

"I agree," a voice nearby said. "I destroyed Baghdad with Hulagu Khan and you don't see the Persians whining."

"There are no Persians anymore," I said, turning to him.

Greeting me was the oldest vampire I'd ever met, probably the oldest vampire most people would ever meet. The Second Eldest,

Enil—or Eddie, as he liked to be called—was a full-on Orlock-looking vampire. Actually, he made Count Orlock look like *People's* Sexiest Man Alive.

Eddie had skin so sunken and scaly it looked almost reptilian. All of his hair had fallen out. His nose had disappeared, only to be replaced with slits, and his fingers were twice as long as a normal human being's. His teeth were sharpened to shark-like fangs, making him appear vaguely animal-like. I couldn't sense his strength at all, which was probably a good thing since he'd undoubtedly be able to be sensed across the state.

The Second Eldest was dressed in a black sackcloth-like robe that resembled Uncle Fester's attire. It was covered in pockets and had no real fashion to it but gave a striking insight into Eddie's inner life. A Kindle, three different cellphones, an iPad, several sets of keys, and what looked like a pile of coins were all visible inside them. There was also a bookmarked copy of *Salem's Lot*. I'd say Eddie was an eccentric-looking vampire, but when you've outlived Christianity four times, you're really able to live however you want, even if you look like an exceptionally well-wired homeless man.

If any vampire was capable of killing Renaud, it was the Second Eldest. It was something of a mystery why he'd chosen to live in New Detroit unlike most ancients, accepting only a position on the City Council versus ruling the entirety of the United States as his personal territory.

"Really?" Eddie said, covering his heart. "Such a shame. They were such a sweet and tasty people."

"Right," I said, trying to figure out how to broach the subject. "So, Eddie, how ya enjoying the party?"

"It's dead," Eddie said, laughing as if it were funny. "I swear, these kind of crappy parties are why I left the Old Country. I love this new artificial blood, though. When you reach my age, one rat is enough to sustain you for a decade, but I could drink this all day."

"Uh, Eddie, we need to talk." I looked to Thoth.

Thoth, clearly nervous, started speaking. "Second Eldest, we beseech you to aid us in a combating a dire threat to the whole of—"

"I've stopped listening," Eddie said, waving his hand. "Go away."

"We want you to help us kill Renaud," I said.

Eddie looked back up. "Okay, sure, that sounds fun. Why didn't you just say so?"

"Fun?" Thoth managed to choke out.

"Oh yes," Eddie said. "We always used to host big Wild Hunts with the Unseelie Lords, Gods of the Dead, and Odin whenever we found Lamia's other god-botherer spawn. You newborns these days have no idea what's it like having to try and root out every Elder God cult in the world. Millions of dead, hundreds of destroyed civilizations, and all to make sure some asshole doesn't bring about the end of the world. At least with the Crucifixians, they're willing to wait for their god to come back and wipe out everything. There's got to be at least one religion not looking forward to the end of everything, right? Tell me one has arisen."

"Uh, Wicca?" I suggested.

"Oh, good," Eddie said. "There's hope for humanity yet. Yes, I'll help you kill Renaud. We'll need a couple of more Old Ones to help, though. He-he, Old Ones. I swear, you kids today and your nicknames to make you sound all badass. I can probably kill Renaud, but backup would be good. Who knows what the Dreamers have given him over the years."

"Thank you," I said, nodding my head.

Thoth just looked confused.

"We black vampires have to stick together," Eddie said, punching me in the shoulder.

"Uh, right." I had not known he was black.

Eddie sauntered away, leaving the two of us alone.

"You blew it, T," I said, chuckling. "I don't think he's a big man for ceremony."

"He's as close to a human-shaped volcano as exists," Thoth said.

"Are you sure you're not projecting?"

"Better to be safe than sorry."

The thought of getting Eddie on our side for hunting down Renaud gave me a sense of confidence we could pull this off. I could feel Melissa's distress in the back of my mind, horrible worry and self-loathing mixed with a desire to stop her creator no matter the cost. I was bonded with her now—it was something I couldn't deny anymore—and I was ready to do anything to save her. I just needed some more people powerful enough to help me do it.

"So, we've got one member of our little vigilante posse," I said, looking at Thoth. "Who else can we recruit?"

"Fatimah is an automatic yes. Even if she wasn't my creation, she's been hunting Renaud for decades."

"Personal or professional?" I asked.

"Both," Thoth said. "Every one of Renaud's victims was someone loved by someone."

"I trust her," I said. "We could try to get Mama Kali, but I don't know if she's up for violence against Elisha and her group."

"So you admit the Network is involved?" Thoth said. "And are no longer protecting them?"

I frowned at him. "Is this an 'I told you so'?"

"Absolutely."

"Yeah, they're a bunch of psychos now. Because you and the other Old Ones drove them to it."

"Evil is always a choice," Thoth said. "Even if you're pushed into it, you still have to take the final step yourself."

"Thank you, Yoda."

"Eddie is closer to our Yoda."

"Hey, I think he looks great for eight thousand. But, seriously, we need another heavy hitter or two."

"Thoth, I need you to look at these shoes. Do they look like legitimate Jimmy Choos or imitators?" Voivode Ashura spoke from a few feet. "They feel slightly off. If they're knockoffs, heads will roll."

I turned to look at the spectacularly dressed red-headed vampire monarch of New Detroit. She was wearing an expensive crimson dress that managed to leave quite a bit to the imagination but was only more enticing for it.

"She's our best bet," Thoth said, turning around.

"Are you kidding me?" I asked.

"Not at all." Thoth bowed before his fiancée. "My lady, we have a request to make."

Oh Lord.

CHAPTER TWENTY-ONE

"So, let me get this straight. You want me, the ruler of the richest city in the Vampire Nation, to join you on the battlefield against Renaud, the most powerful vampire hunter in the world. Because, in part, you think he's a continuing threat to New Detroit, but mostly to save your girlfriend." Voivode Ashura's summation wasn't flattering, but it wasn't inaccurate either. "Do I have that right?"

"She's not my girlfriend," I said, trying to figure out if that made it better or worse.

Ashura's eyes were pitying. "Given you had a whole evening with her after her creation, then you clearly were doing something wrong."

"Vampires really have some strange ideas about dating," I muttered, ashamed.

"If you're attracted to someone, fuck and eat them. What's so strange about that?" Ashura shrugged her dainty little shoulders.

I had no answer for that. "So, you won't help us?"

"Well, it's been a while since I was a magistrate, but I see no reason not to."

"You were a magistrate?" I believed Fatimah was one, but had difficulty imagining Turkish Milla Jovovich here as one of the Council's hatchet-men.

"I was born in the harem of my father to a slave girl he'd purchased from Irish traders. I was sold then to a vampire who intended to make me a concubine for eternity. In order to escape that kind of life, you need to learn to fight and kill, because at the end of the day, that's the only way anyone gets out of the worst situations."

I'd have argued Doctor King, but I'd always been a Malcolm X sort of guy anyway. Plus I didn't want to argue with someone who was doing me a favor. "Well, thank you very much for taking this risk."

"Why wouldn't I do anything for family?" Ashura smiled and reached over to pinch one of my cheeks.

I took a step back so she couldn't touch me. "Uh, I just thought—"

Ashura paused. "I don't think I could ever convince you Eaton was once a good man after what he did to you."

"You're damned right."

Ashura looked down. "However, he made me happy once. Why he became so consumed with destroying those weaker than himself and toadying to those stronger is a mystery we will perhaps never solve."

"He tasted of the sun and life in your lips, my lady," Thoth explained. "When he could no longer do so, blood became ash in his mouth and the night became a shroud of horror and loneliness."

"By which you mean it wasn't at all my fault and I should just move on, right?" Ashura said, sniffing a bit as if ready to cry.

"Of course," Thoth said.

Ashura kissed him on the cheek.

"If you'll excuse me, I have to go get my katana," Ashura said cheerfully. "Also change into a pair of boots. These shoes are completely inappropriate for combat."

I watched her walk off, still not sure I'd actually seen anything that had just happened. "Please tell me I don't have to call her 'Mom.'"

"No promises," Thoth said.

"I swear, vampires just get weirder every day."

"It'll get worse before it gets better."

"When does it get better?"

"I'll tell you when it happens."

I gave a short chuckle before looking over my shoulder suspiciously. There was a chill running up and down my spine. It was a sensation of dread I hadn't felt since my brother's death. I couldn't shake it and it was making me feel every bit as queasy as the sunlit room had.

"Is something wrong?" Thoth asked.

"Remember how the first half of *From Dusk Till Dawn* is a generic crime thriller and then bam, it's suddenly a vampire movie where almost the entire cast gets slaughtered?"

"The only thing I remember from that movie is Salma Hayek dancing."

I grinned, remembering that myself. "Yeah, well, I can't shake the feeling we're all about to become lunch."

"Going after Renaud, even with the help we've got, is close to suicide. After all, we haven't told everyone about his army of Network spies you told me he wasn't assembling."

"Yeah, well … wait, you knew?"

"Yeah, it's not like I can read your thoughts or anything."

I glared at him. "Why'd you go with it?"

"You never will get that you're my family, will you?"

I frowned. "Why is that, man? I surely can't be the first guy like me you've met over the centuries."

Thoth looked down. "I'm surprised you haven't figured it out by now, Peter. Doubye didn't take me to kill my family immediately after changing me. He kept me prisoner with his powers for a decade and a half. My son was a man by the time I killed him. He was a soldier and a defender of the weak like you, even if also a bit of a scoundrel."

It was something he'd never confessed to me before. "I know this is meant to be a touching moment and all, but does that mean I'm just your replacement goldfish?"

Thoth stared at me. "I am never telling you anything personal ever again."

"Man, I already know you Old Ones spend your mornings as lethargic insomniacs watching DVDs and playing video games. There's nowhere to go but up after that."

"I don't remember what vampires did before television, I admit," Thoth chuckled.

"I read," Fatimah said, walking up to join us.

Fatimah was still wearing attire that made her look like a hypothetical villainess in the next *Underworld* movie. She was wearing a mixed leather and Kevlar outfit that somehow was still practical despite being far, far too form-fitting. Was it magic, an illusion, or just ridiculously flexible for armor?

"Oh, hey—"

Fatimah raised her hand. "Not yet. I'm too busy dealing with the fact Dracu-Barbie has told me she's my mother now and we're going to kill Renaud."

"Yeah, that's about the size of it," Thoth said. "Peter can sense Renaud through the vampire hunter."

"Her name is Melissa," I said.

My head started hurting as I saw flashes of cars driving across a road. It was territory I didn't recognize, but I sensed it was Melissa and Renaud. My connection with her had to have been strong because usually telepathy didn't travel very far.

Fatimah frowned. "You don't understand what you're dealing with here, Thoth, Peter. Renaud is not the kind of vampire you can just gather a lynch mob to go kill."

"Please don't talk about lynching," I said, rubbing my temples.

"I can use it better than most since my father was hanged," Fatimah said, continuing. "You need to let the professionals handle it."

"As you've handled it over the past seven hundred years?" Thoth said, frowning.

Fatimah glared. "What the hell is that supposed to mean."

"I'm saying that the Council of Ancients has done an extremely poor job of actually dealing with Renaud. You're the only one, I suspect, who takes hunting him down seriously, and you shouldn't down any help you can get."

Fatimah glared. "Oh, is that how it's supposed to be. I come back into your life and it's back to being under your rules, is it? Do you know how many decades it took to establish my own identity after we parted?"

Thoth frowned at her. "I can count the years from World War II, Fatimah. It hasn't been so long since you, I, and Lucinda fought the Nazi Geistopo program."

Okay, that was a story which needed clarification.

"I am twice the warrior you ever were. Both you and Ashura have been out of the game for far too long to think you can just jump right back in. Besides, you were an assassin-for-hire, not a magistrate, and that is two very different skill sets."

The headache was blinding now and I couldn't see anything but

Melissa's vision of the road they were taking … right to the airport.

Oh hell.

"We have the Second Eldest coming with us," Thoth said, his voice overlaying the vision I was receiving.

"Oh, because that's a brilliant idea. Let's put the vampire who absorbs the power of other vampires with his magic sword in the same room with the most powerful one alive!"

"And he'll keep getting more powerful unless we stop—"

"He's here," I whispered. "They're all here."

I could sense more of the situation now. There was a convoy of Army Humvees moving down the road and parking on the tarmac right before an illusion-covered staircase that led to the underground compound where we were presently located. I saw a small army of Network forces present, and Renaud got through the wards on the steel door simply by pointing at it and saying, "Open."

Causing the door to explode.

That was when the vision ended and there was a combination of noises happening at once. First, an alarm was going off around the room, interrupting "Once Bitten" by Three Speed (a.k.a. the theme song to a young Jim Carrey's vampire comedy with Lauren Hutton).

This didn't seem to affect the Ancients and Old Ones around me, though, as they started moving around the room sluggishly. The second noise might have been responsible for the effect, as all the silver statues around the room started singing.

"That's not normal," I said, plugging my ears.

I looked over to Eddie, who had fallen over on the ground, not dead but not moving. Thoth zipped to his side, then checked his cup of artificial blood.

"Is it poisoned?" Fatimah asked, losing all of her earlier condescension.

Thoth tossed it aside. "Worse. Enchanted. The spell only activates in combination with the statue. The artificial blood was delivered through trustworthy sources, though."

Fatimah growled. "Ex-Network."

"Like you said, revenge is a dish best served cold," I muttered. "And we've been Worfed."

"How the hell did they find us?" Fatimah pulled out her cellphone and started calling someone before zipping to all the doors around the room, shutting them one by one.

Thoth looked at me. "Apparently, while we were planning to use Melissa's mind to read his mind, he was using her to read yours."

I let that sink in. "*Son of a bitch*. He played us."

"He played you," Fatimah said, appearing by my side. "We need to get everyone to the evacuation point."

Ashura arrived from a connecting room, having changed into a bouncy pink dress down to her ankles and a pair of bright red combat boots that made me wonder where the hell she'd kept a change of clothing. The fact that she also had a Muramasa katana (Thoth had taught me to tell the difference between types, and this was the Evil Excalibur type) completed the surreal image.

"It may be too late for that," Ashura said. "They're going through our defenses like—well, like you'd expect. We need to revive whoever hasn't been drinking the cheap-ass blood, presumably the non-Ancient of the group, and get them armed. Thoth, I know you're a fighter, but you're also the only mage in this group. I need you to try and break the spell on the statues if you can, or at least suppress it."

"Some explosives would be good for a start," Thoth said.

"Consider it done. We need to also get what Ancients we can away from the battlefield even if not evacuated," Ashura said, pointing to a trio of young women and men with model-level looks whom I recognized as her other children. They were all armed, making it look like the *Vogue* militia. "Any Old Ones who see a prone Ancient might be inclined to take some revenge or create an opening in the power structure. I'm a bit tempted myself, but if you mention that to anyone else, I'll kill you. Fatimah, are you prepared?"

"Who put you in charge?" Fatimah said, crossing her arms.

"This is *my* city." Ashura bared her fangs.

Fatimah bared hers back.

"Ladies, you're both pretty," I said, trying to keep the peace. "Could we—"

Both hissed at me and I wanted to hide behind Thoth. "Right. I'll just, uh, be over here. Crying."

One of the fashion model vampires, a devastatingly good-looking black man named Gerald, tossed me my shotgun. Apparently, they'd recovered that from where I'd been disabled at the Burgertown. I

started moving bodies left and right down to the janitors' closet
even as I caught images from Melissa's eyes of Renaud slaughtering
the PMC soldiers who were protecting the place. He was invading
the place damn near single-handedly, but sometimes tossed guards
back to his people or sent them to adjoining rooms to massacre
everyone.

I'd seen close, methodical, and efficient commanders before.
Renaud was just a butcher.

About halfway through, having managed to revive six or seven
Old Ones, I felt a clawed hand grab me by the ankle.

"Ah!" I shouted, turning my shotgun around.

It was Eddie, using me to climb to his feet. "All right, now I'm
pissed."

"You're awake," I said, surprised, as all the other Ancients were
dead to the world.

"One second," Eddie said, vomiting up a literal gallon of blood
on the floor, utterly spraying my shoes and legs.

"That's nasty," I said, staring.

He threw up some more and then wiped his mouth, surrounded
by a gigantic puddle of blood. His clothes were covered in it.

"I'm good now," Eddie said. "What's going on?"

"Siege," I said. "Bad guys about to arrive."

Eddie nodded. "Good, good. In my day, it was always a dull
party without at least three murders."

"You were Dothraki."

"Love that show!" Eddie said, cheerfully. "I watch it with my
grandkids along with my morning soaps. Can't watch at it at night,
too scary for them. Did you see what happened to Stannis's little—"

Any further inane conversation was interrupted by the sound of
a muted explosion echoing through the chamber. The lights in the
room shifted from brilliant fluorescent white to an ominous shade
of red.

"What was that?" Fatimah asked, moving the last of the Ancients
over her shoulder.

"I had every explosive but the ones Thoth requested packed in
the room before the entrance," Ashura said, giving a black smile.
"It required sacrificing the remainder of the security personnel, but
that should weaken our foe."

"Those were our men!" Fatimah hissed.

"And this is war!" Ashura snapped back.

I felt a wave of nausea pass over me as I saw through Melissa's eyes the sight of a long metal hallway filled with choking amounts of human ash and flame. Renaud was little more than a fleshy skeleton standing up with his bone sword in one bony hand. Worse, I myself—or Melissa, in this case—had also been struck by the bomb. I should have been killed instantly, but Renaud was keeping her alive and holding back the pain. He was powerful enough to lend her his power even as both regenerated. as if being caught in the middle of a massive explosion was nothing more than an inconvenience.

Ah, hell.

Elisha, who had been at the back of the group, was unharmed. She moved up to join Renaud, only for him to backhand her away while his flesh returned to normal and even his hair regrew. He was soon a very large, pissed-off naked man with a bone sword. Worse, he was right outside the door.

Renaud then pointed to it and commanded it to open.

Which it did.

CHAPTER TWENTY-TWO

Renaud and his army poured forth like a plague from the door, the naked sword-wielding vampire slicing through a business-suit-wearing Old One who exploded into ashes before Renaud bounded past him. Behind Renaud was an equally naked Melissa, man-sized werewolves, snake-headed lizardmen, and worse.

There was also Elisha. She was wearing the exact outfit she'd been wearing earlier, only having added a Kevlar vest and carrying an anti-material rifle. I didn't know how to react to her, but I knew she'd come to kill me and everyone here.

So I had to kill her.

That was when the silver statues all around the room exploded, showering the attackers with pieces of silver. The eerie music vanished, only to be replaced by DJ BoBo's "Vampires are Alive," which made me think the DJ for tonight's music had to be the lamest of all time.

Thoth made an incantation, calling on all the suddenly released magic and unleashing a storm of black lightning that tore into the attackers as the remaining vampires on the ground stirred. Ashura and Fatimah leapt forward, cutting into the attackers one after the other with katana and a shadow formed into a battle-ax.

Much to my surprise, I also saw Jumping Jack Flash and Mama Kali join the fray with a number of renegade (loyalist? our guys? I don't know what to call them) Network agents I recognized but didn't know well. Kali knocked away bullets as they sailed at her, only to turn the nearest of the Network attackers into bloody mincemeat with swords that sliced through bone like gelatin.

"Sorry guys," I muttered, watching one of the snake-things run up to me and go for my face, only for me to dodge out of the way and lift my shotgun behind its head before firing. It exploded into ashes when its head came mostly off. Another came after me and suffered a similar fate.

I started fighting my way toward Melissa, firing my shotgun over and over. I pumped it, fired, fired, and fired again before re-pumping it. I never had to reload the weapon, as it fed the number of people I killed. I targeted those Network soldiers trying to feed on the Old Ones on the ground we hadn't evacuated. I usually wounded them rather than killing them, but I was able to prove a bit of a distraction before the next monster tried to kill me.

I tried to take a couple of shots at Renaud, but the Network soldiers threw themselves in front of the blasts even though they wouldn't do much damage to the naked sword-swinger. His ritual to empower them with his blood had made them all but puppets. He was using them to strike out with impunity, and I had to wonder how much better this fight would have been going for him if he didn't just send them out to their deaths.

Renaud charged at Enil, and the Second Eldest blocked the Tooth of Azazel with two hideous sword-shaped bone protrusions that jutted from the base of his elbows. The sword cut through them one at a time, only for the Second Eldest to regenerate and strike again. Ashura, Kali, and Fatimah carved their way to support him, but Renaud severed off the Ancient One's arm, then struck off Ashura's.

As this occurred, the already-diminished army of fifty Network soldiers turned rapidly to an army of twenty-five, then twenty. Some of the Old Ones on the ground rose to do battle to defend themselves—lethargically. This only delayed the inevitable. I saw one of Ashura's children, a beautiful Spanish woman in a blood-splattered dress fighting with a pair of pistols, disintegrate as her head disappeared from a sniper rifle shot from Elisha.

Elisha then aimed her rifle at Thoth.

"No!" I shouted, knocking two werewolves feasting on a screaming Old One on the ground before shooting at Elisha.

Much to my horror, Melissa leapt in front of the blow and took it head on. Most of her chest was destroyed and the sight that greeted me was a feral monster. Renaud had stripped away her dignity and sanity, using her as a weapon in this fight just as he was using everyone else. In her right hand was a polished metal stake, and I could tell she planned to drive it in me. Another night and I might have welcomed it, but she was standing in the way of me and Elisha.

"I command you to be yourself again," I said, not at all thinking that would work.

Melissa stared at me, hissed, then turned around to stab Elisha right through the heart with the stake for the second time that night.

"Bitch!" Elisha called out, coughing blood and dropping her rifle on the ground.

I stared at the woman I once thought I might have loved, then waved my hand. "Bye Elisha."

Melissa snapped Elisha's neck for good measure.

"I really hate that woman," Melissa hissed through fangs that impeded her speech.

I was too busy shooting the werewolves who tried to sucker punch me from behind to respond to that.

"She had a good side, once." I remembered when we'd met at the supernatural unemployment office, where she'd been working as a temp.

"Where did she leave it?" Melissa asked, picking up the anti-material rifle and firing it into Renaud's back twice.

Renaud seemed mildly perturbed by it.

"Old Detroit," I said, suddenly feeling a gale force wind's edge as Thoth summoned a powerful spell that sent all of Renaud's remaining soldiers flying through the air. They slammed against the wall, disabled, giving the remaining Old Ones on the ground a chance to rise.

Which they promptly used to flee, abandoning us to Renaud.

Thanks, guys. Really.

The remainder of the renegade Network soldiers ran to the disabled attackers in order to finish us off, leaving Renaud and the few remaining individuals to fight. Much to my surprise, Voivode Ashura was still fighting despite having only one arm and a broken sword. She was covered in blood and had a thoroughly pissed-off look on her face.

Fatimah looked exhausted, her body covered in bloody sweat even as she still had her shadow swords drawn. Kali was lying on the ground, unconscious with blood coming from the base of her head. It was probably a good thing the Old Ones had fled, since I couldn't imagine one wouldn't have taken advantage of her prone position.

Jumping Jack Flash had the worst of it, as he'd been bisected by Renaud's sword. He wasn't a vampire, though, so he was trying to plug together his various severed organs so they'd regenerate. It was both comical and horrifying in that *Herbert West: ReAnimator* sort of way. I didn't see the Second Eldest and briefly thought he'd fled or been killed before I saw a horde of rats feeding on corpses.

Eddie was regaining his strength.

Renaud didn't look the slightest bit injured, his powers having allowed him to recover from everything Thoth and the others had dished out to him. Instead, the naked knight took a moment to look among us. "I must say, you are perhaps the most determined vampires I have ever met. I fully expected to meet heavy resistance, but only from the Old Ones and Ancients trying to fight for their lives. You actually seem like you're willing to risk yourselves for something else. It's tragic, really, that it's such an evil cause as this city."

Voivode Ashura stared at Renaud with pure hatred in her eyes. "Do you think I like living as a parasite? Killing to survive, moving from city to city, never able to stay too long? For centuries, I tried to create companions who would love me, but they always reacted with fear and hatred because they didn't know the consequences of what I was asking of them. This city represents a chance for our kind to move past the horrors and embrace the light, even if it's a neon casino light instead of the sun. I will not let you destroy it and my few friends in this world."

Wait, she had friends?

Probably best not to bring that up.

Fatimah also displayed her contempt. "Individuals like you know nothing of true suffering."

"What?" Renaud scowled, displaying his fangs. "How dare you! My suffering is beyond compare save the Lord's own son."

Strangely, his comparison of himself to Jesus didn't cause me any distress. Perhaps because the Lord knew it was horseshit.

"Do you think murdering vampires makes up for your other sins?" Fatimah scoffed. "I have studied you for years and charted your course across Europe. You murder those you deem to be sinners, rape any woman who strikes your fancy, and use people before discarding them like refuse. Then you wrap it all in religion and claim you were doing the Lord's work. God Almighty, you live up to your Knight Templar brethren's example and exceed them."

Renaud sniffed the air. "I would not expect an apostate Moor to understand such matters."

"You use the fang of a damn demon god!" I snapped at him. "I'm pretty sure that's against one of the commandments."

"The first, actually," Melissa said.

"You hear her? The first commandment!" I snapped. "No coveting or shit. The first!"

Why was I taunting the invincible super-vampire?

This wasn't a good idea.

Renaud just glared at me. "You? You will die first."

Yeah, that was a terrible idea.

I shrugged. "I'd say Blade wanted his wardrobe back too, but you're kind of not wearing anything, Smalls."

He actually wasn't. I was even kind of jealous, but insulting a man's dick was the surest way to get him to do something stupid. Unfortunately, doing something stupid seemed to be charging up at me with his sword.

I shot Renaud three times in the chest, to almost no effect, slowing him down only a bit before I managed to barely avoid his first strike. Melissa fired her weapon at point-blank range, only for Renaud to reach out and cut it in half with a single blow.

"Die, Demon," Renaud said, knocking me across the face with the pommel of his blade before knocking me to the ground and putting his foot on my throat. He was starting to bleed from his forehead, at last starting to look tired as he regenerated from the rifle shot in his chest.

Thoth grabbed Renaud around the neck, shouting something in French, which probably was something like, "Get the hell away from creation, you bitch."

Renaud just ripped him off his back and then stabbed him through the chest with the Tooth of Azazel.

Thoth screamed.

I felt the pain as he started dying.

Then time stood still.

"Oh, now you kick in!" I said, shouting at the universe. "When it's worthless!"

I pulled out my kukri and stabbed Renaud a dozen times in the chest, trying to strike out at the figure that had killed my best friend and was now striking at my creator. It didn't give me a sense of actually harming him, though.

Until Melissa looked right at me. "The Tooth of Azazel. Use it."

I stared down at the evil weapon buried in Thoth. It radiated an evil unnatural energy that defied the supernatural stillness all around me. I hadn't believed much in God while alive, and while I did while dead, I didn't really feel like relying on him. I did, however, think using that weapon would be against his will.

Too bad.

Pulling out the Tooth of Azazel and ripping it from Renaud's grip, I saw time return to normal a second before the blow connected. Renaud's eyes widened right before he tried to move out of the way. His movement was slowed though by the bone knife in his chest and his head went flying off his shoulders.

Renaud's body fell on its knees, then turned to ashes.

He was dead at last.

"There can be only one," I muttered.

Melissa, Fatima, and Ashura stared at me.

Falling to one knee, I felt the power of Renaud continue to course through my veins. A red mist moved from Renaud's ashes up into my chest, then in and out of my veins. I felt it changing my blood in ways both surreal and unthinkable. I could feel myself becoming more powerful by the second as I saw flashes from the lives of the hundreds of vampires Renaud had destroyed over the past seven centuries.

A nun in Medieval Bologna who was desperate to pray away the sins she'd committed both upon her fellow sisters and against the animals of the forest.

An arrogant Victorian aristocrat who considered humans cattle and routinely killed his servants before replacing them with other poor desperate souls.

A Syrian conqueror and warlord who had laid waste to thousands of souls on the battlefield during his mortal life only to kill even more behind the scenes upon his immortality.

A veterinarian who never harmed any man, woman, or child in her entire immortal life of six hundred years.

Oscar Wilde.

Wait, Oscar Wilde?

God damn you, Renaud!

Thoth lay on the ground, not moving. He was bleeding badly from the wound in his stomach. You could tell how bad a wound it was because, as I mentioned before, vampires don't bleed. The Tooth of Azazel had caused him to become a virtual oil strike of vampire blood, though, and it wasn't healing. If the wound itself didn't kill him, I was sure one of the ravenous angry Old Ones around me would finish him off.

Thoth reached up to me with his trembling hand. "You did it, Peter. You did it. Now I die at—"

I slapped him. "Stay with me, Thoth! I am not letting this turn into a touching tragic scene! You will stay with me or I will go to Hell and beat your jewelry-store-running ass!"

Thoth actually laughed at that, despite the pain.

Melissa put her hand on my shoulder. "Peter—"

"Let me do this!" I shouted, trying to figure out something to do to save my creator. I had an idea. It wasn't a good idea, but it sounded like it might work in theory. At least if I did it quickly enough.

The daughter of Violette Szabo who helped her undead mother slaughter Nazis wherever they could.

A Spanish exorcist who wandered around the world casting out demons while feeding on the blood of the Eucharist, made real by the strength of his faith.

A pair of transsexuals who'd fought to protect their people from those who would slaughter them.

"Bite me," I said, looking down at Thoth.

"Excuse me?" Thoth said.

"Do it!" I said, feeling the transformation's final stage beginning. "Before it's too late."

"But if I can't stop, I'll—"

"Do it!" I shouted again.

Thoth pushed forward and grabbed me before sinking his fangs into my neck. I won't talk about how it felt, as it was awkward enough with my being heterosexual, Thoth being my father figure, and my trying to save his life by risking my own. Thoth grabbed me by the shoulders and I felt some of the enhanced blood flow from my blood into his body as the power transferring to me started transferring to him as well.

That was when I passed out.

If I was going out like this, well, it was worth it.

EPILOGUE

I woke up in a closed coffin. Huh, that was new. Contrary to popu-lar media depictions, vampires didn't sleep in coffins unless they were trying to be too hip for their own good. I mean, yeah, they had a snug comfort to them and great back support, but that wasn't enough to justify sleeping in them. I was also wearing a brand new suit, which was something I'd missed even though it added to the "Am I attending my own funeral?" feel.

Pushing open the top part of the coffin lid, I was pleased to note I hadn't been buried alive. That had happened to me once as a kind of undead fraternity prank, and I wasn't anxious to repeat the experience. I was in a pleasant little marble-floored room. It was empty but for a giant pentagram surrounding my coffin along with a set of candles made of animal fat on metal stands. I recognized it as a spell designed to help vampires transitioning to Old One status compartmentalize all of their newfound power. I wondered why they'd stored me in it. Probably they'd just run out of space with all the other recovering vampires.

Fluorescent lights were on above my head, and I was feeling surprisingly rejuvenated. Better than rejuvenated, in fact. Hell, I would dare say I felt awesome, and that was a rare feeling when you were undead. Then I remembered David was dead. Still, Renaud was dead and that made it better. Somewhat. A little. Maybe if I kept telling myself that. Pretending I wasn't hurting, I decided to try something. Pushing the rest of the coffin lid off, I lay back down in the coffin.

"Children of the night, what music they make. Fear not, your master arises!" I stretched out my arms straight and tried to levitate myself up without bending my back. I managed to do it, only to slip back down and fall in the coffin as soon as I finished.

Dammit, almost had it. Interestingly, I noticed my body was lighter before and levitating was much easier. Closing my eyes, I lifted myself up in the air and found myself smacking against the ceiling very quickly. I then concentrated on going to the right and ended up smacking myself against the wall beside the door. I did a couple of back rolls and barrel flips in the air before initially shouting. "Holy crap, I'm flying!"

Not levitation.

Not floating.

Real, actual, honest-to-Devil flight!

The door to the room opened up and I stopped concentrating on my flight to look. I immediately smacked against the ground, landing with a thud. OK, that was another thing I needed to be wary of. Flying required a lot more concentration than floating. It was Thoth again, wearing a pair of blue jeans and a white cotton button-down shirt. It was his working attire, and I could smell the incense, Saint John's wort, blood, and chemicals, which were signs he'd been hard at spell-work.

"Hey Gandalf," I said, smiling. "Glad to see you're still alive."

"The same in return," Thoth said, smiling. "You realize we usually practice flying outdoors, correct?"

"Oh, hush you," I said, sounding like my mother. "What's going on? Did I get a portion of Renaud's powers?"

Thoth nodded. "More than a portion, I'd say. You saved my life back there, and I gained a bit of Renaud's strength myself from you."

I tried not to remember the feelings I'd had as he'd bit me. "Yeah, let's never speak of that again. Except, well, how much?"

"I dare say my power has doubled."

"Useful for your honeymoon."

"Victoria is incensed about her arm and probably the fact our marriage contract is going to have to be renegotiated since we're approximate equals now. Still, she's enjoying the fact she's a hero for killing the infamous Renaud."

"Fatimah didn't get credit?" I asked.

"She's only a hundred and fifty years old, so she's been regulated to a minor supporting player in the drama, magistrate or not."

I grinned. "I bet she loved that."

"It teaches the valuable life lesson of 'If you want respect, make sure it's from people whom you actually should give a crap about the opinion of'—which the Ancients are manifestly not." On the plus side, she's been given a new mission to destroy the Tooth of Azazel."

"She should dump the sword into a volcano."

"My suggestion."

I paused, thinking about how I felt. "Have I gotten stronger?"

"You could say that."

"How much stronger?" I asked, not at all eager.

"Stronger than me," Thoth said, walking over and offering me a hand.

"So I'm an Old One now? Immortal and shit?"

"Not in the slightest," Thoth said. "You have the potential for a much stronger vampire's abilities, but none of the training that would allow you to master them all. Plus, you're still not immortal to regular humans and accidents. That, it seems, only comes with age."

I took his hand and stood up. "Well, that's a bummer."

"Yes, you're just totally being cheated here," Thoth said, playfully sarcastic. "I do think you're not going to have to worry about the G-word anymore, though."

"God?" I said, without irony. "Ha! Jesus! Michael Jordan! Santa! Odin!"

"Stop that, please," Thoth said.

"The Prophets of Bajor! Eru! Aslan! Link the Hero of Time! Mario!"

"I think you're stretching the Chosen One metaphor."

"Anakin Skywalker was a virgin birth. He counts."

"Those movies don't count and you know it," Thoth said. "Either way, you've done a great service, and we were even able to finish what the meeting was all about. The Vampire Nation is now owner of the majority of North Dakota's oil fields."

"There's oil in North Dakota?" I asked. "How much?"

"A great deal," Thoth said. "You have no idea how difficult it was to cover it up for as long as we have. It won't fix all of our bankruptcy issues, and there are a lot of dead bodies thanks to it, but both the United States as well as its undead residents may get through this financial crisis intact now."

I looked at him. "Thoth, don't take this the wrong way, but I could not give less of a shit about how much money you guys make."

Thoth gave a half-smile. "I understand."

I kept my gaze even. "How many died?"

"On our side? Seven vampires total. Four Old Ones and three Ancients. A catastrophic loss by all accounts, but it could have been much worse. The Vampire Nation owes you a debt of gratitude and the Council, for all its faults, never forgets its debts."

"How many humans?" I asked, not reacting in the slightest.

Thoth paused. "Fifty-seven. We don't know how many renegade Network soldiers came to fight Elisha's group, but I'm guessing they lost around ten or twelve. I think out of a group of twenty."

"What's being done for them?" I asked.

"Terrorists are being blamed for the attack with a few dozen bodies of their membership being transported here so it looks like an attack on the godless demons that America is protecting. It'll be national news alongside the Human Rights League bombing for probably the next week until someone famous adopts a baby or another celebrity decides to transition to being a vampire."

"I meant to honor their sacrifice."

Thoth closed his eyes. "I will provide their families with enough money to never want for security again."

"So, nothing that wasn't you."

"No."

"Figures." I didn't know why I'd expected anything different. "What about survivors on Renaud's side?"

"After Renaud died, the remainder surrendered. That was their mistake, as they've been sent to spend the rest of their lives as meals for the Ancients as punishment. Only Melissa and Elisha will be spared."

The latter part surprised me. "Why Elisha?"

"Her father is a very prominent vampire in Washington, D.C., and we require his assistance. He's asked for clemency and she's to spend the next ten years in a box. Ashura traded her to him for help in covering all this up. Also, to negotiate for Kali's Network not to be slaughtered to the man."

"That was nice of her," I said, trying to think of how horrible it was for Elisha to be returned to the man she despised most in the world. I considered rescuing her from him, but I didn't know if I could because if she did escape him, I'd have to kill her. She didn't deserve a pardon for what she'd done, even if she didn't deserve what the Vampire Nation had in store for her.

"Ashura believes you can catch more flies with honey and wants the Network to help populate Milwaukee, Chicago, Pittsburgh, Cleveland, and Saint Louis with supernaturals. There's a power vacuum there she wants to fill."

"And Melissa?"

"She's been given a full pardon for her crimes, although I don't think the Council of Ancients has any idea of the real extent of her actions with Renaud. I'm all right with keeping it that way. Because of her experience with the religious right and her somewhat clean-cut inoffensive image, I've also suggested she form a Human-Vampire Friendship League with herself at the head."

"Even though we're incredibly non-friendly."

Thoth smiled. "She's asked about you."

I gave a half-smile. "You think a princess and a guy like me—"

"I predict six months of passionate sex and ardor followed by arguing and a regret-filled breakup."

"Ah."

"But those will be a glorious six months."

I smiled. "I'll give it a shot then."

I thought about Melissa and tried to reach out to contact her. Much to my surprise, it was very easy. I could sense everyone outside of the room for about half a mile. It required a bit of sorting, but it meant Thoth hadn't been lying about me being much stronger. I had a real 'Professor Xavier and Cerebro thing' going on as I searched out Melissa through our still-intact bond.

In the end, I found her awake and looking over documents in a nearby conference room. We were still underground in the airport bunker, but the majority of the place was covered in police tape as the police were fed a heaping pack of lies by the undead. I could feel Melissa's disgust at the proceedings even as she was also feeling an immense amount of relief at Renaud's death.

Uhm, hey, I said to her mentally.

Oh, Peter, thank God you're alive.

You doubted it?

A little bit. They took your body away immediately after you fell unconscious. I was wondering if they were experimenting on you or something. Praise Jes—er, I mean, Praise the J-man.

No, it's okay, I'm apparently immune now.

Oh, that's good.

I don't know if I'll be attending Sunday church with Grandmother Stone, but it's about the only benefit of this.

Yeah, Melissa said back to me. *I was such a fool to fall for Renaud's tricks.*

I think you literally didn't have a choice.

I had a choice in the beginning, Melissa said. *I can tell the difference between having my mind bent and just attraction.*

Then you have no taste in men.

Melissa laughed. *OK, that was funny. Did you hear about the job offering?*

Yeah, congratulations.

I'm not sure if I'm going to take it.

I wasn't sure that was actually the sort of job you could refuse. In fact, I was pretty sure the Vampire Nation didn't actually offer much in the way of choice regarding what you did for them. *I think you'd do an amazing job, personally. Besides, it'd be nice to have someone advocating for peace between the sides wanting to kill each other.*

You really think vampires and humans can have peace?

I don't think vampires or humans can have peace with each other, but I think it's worth trying for. It's what every cartoon I watched growing up said was unrealistically easy and just required a big sing-along to achieve.

Uh … huh.

It could happen, I said. *I think you should do it, though.*

Maybe, Melissa said, all but confirming she was going to. I could sense it from her. *I want to go visit my brother first and tell him what I am.*

How do you think he'll react?

A mixture of sympathy and perverse smugness, probably.

So, properly.

Yeah. Melissa paused. *Thank you for helping me get through this, Stone. I don't think I could have done it without you.*

Obviously, because my boss wanted to stake you and leave you out on the roof to burn up.

I could feel Melissa's shock. *I see.*

Say, when you get back, you want to—

Yeah, yeah, I would.

I smiled. *See ya then.*

"Are you done?" Thoth asked.

I nodded. "Yeah, I think we have a shot. I'm going to try to beat that six months."

"Vampires aren't made for eternal devotion, but I wish you luck trying," Thoth said.

"I'll settle for a steady date on Friday nights," I said. "Is there anything else?"

"Quite a bit," Thoth said. "First of all, Eaton's death has left us without a *bellidix*. We need someone to help keep the peace in the city that isn't as corrupt or stupid as the bogatyrs Eaton used."

I paused. "Wait a second, you don't mean?"

"Yes, I do. You have been appointed the new law in town. I'm afraid you're now part of the Man."

I wasn't sure how I felt about that. "Well, at least I can quit my job at the Quick and Shop."

Thoth grimaced. "I should probably mention the job doesn't come with a salary."

"Are you serious?" I snapped.

"I'm sorry," Thoth said. "We'll see your employer compensated so you can take the time off necessary to do your job."

"I hate you. This is all a sick and twisted game, isn't it?"

Thoth smiled. "That which does not kill us—"

"Can go screw itself!"

Thoth pulled out his cellphone and sent a text. "I think this will make the experience much more bearable."

"How do you figure?" I said, too disgusted to look at him now. I couldn't turn down the job any more than Melissa could.

"I put my newfound extra power to use."

David walked through the door, his skin now a shade of gray, the wound across his neck stitched up. He smiled at me. "Hey, Pete, I'm a zombie now!"

ABOUT THE AUTHOR

C.T. Phipps is a lifelong student of horror, science fiction, and fantasy. An avid tabletop gamer, he discovered this passion led him to write and turned him into a lifelong geek. He is a regular blogger and also a reviewer for The Bookie Monster.

Bibliography:

The Rules of Supervillainy (Supervillainy Saga #1)
The Games of Supervillainy (Supervillainy Saga #2)
The Secrets of Supervillainy (Supervillainy Saga #3)
The Science of Supervillainy (Supervillainy Saga #4)
Esoterrorism (Red Room Vol. 1)
Cthulhu Armageddon (Cthulhu Armageddon #1)
The Tower of Zhaal (Cthulhu Armageddon #2)
Lucifer's Star
Straight Outta Fangton

Curious about other Crossroad Press books?
Stop by our site:
http://store.crossroadpress.com
We offer quality writing
in digital, audio, and print formats.

Enter the code FIRSTBOOK
to get 20% off your first order from our store!
Stop by today!